Ellen Burstyn and Charles Grodin in the opening scene.

Same Time, Next Year

A ROMANTIC COMEDY BY

BERNARD SLADE

DELACORTE PRESS

CHARACTERS

GEORGE   A man
DORIS   A woman

SETTING

The entire action of the play takes place in a room
in a traditional country-style inn, two hundred miles
north of San Francisco.

ACT I

Scene 1: A day in February, 1951
Scene 2: A day in February, 1956
Scene 3: A day in February, 1961

ACT II

Scene 1: A day in February, 1965
Scene 2: A day in February, 1970
Scene 3: A day in February, 1975

ACT I

SCENE 1

THE TIME:
A day in February, 1951.

THE PLACE:
A bed-sitting room in the cottage of a country-style inn
near Mendocino, north of San Francisco. The beamed
ceilings, wood-burning fireplace, wallpaper, durable
antique furniture, and burnished brass lamps and fittings
give the setting a feeling of comfortable warmth and
respectable tradition. The room is large enough to contain a
sturdy double bed, chintz-covered sofa and armchairs, and
a baby grand piano. There are two leaded pane glass
windows, a closet door, a door leading to a bathroom and
another door that opens to an outside patio. The room's
aura of permanence is not an illusion. The decor has been
the same for the past twenty-five years and will not change
for the next twenty-five.

AT RISE:
GEORGE and DORIS are asleep in bed. He is twenty-seven
with a likable average face and an intense nervous energy
that gives everything he does a slightly frenetic quality but
doesn't always cover his deep-seated insecurity. Something
wakes him and as he groggily turns over his eyes fall upon
the sleeping form of DORIS beside him. He sits bolt upright
in bed, instantly wide awake.

GEORGE

(*Fervently*)

Oh Jesus.

(*He slips out of bed and we see he is wearing only boxer shorts. He grabs his sports coat from the floor, puts it on and surveys the clothes strewn about the room. They include the rest of his clothes and her blouse, skirt, stockings, bra, girdle, and shoes*)

Jesus H. Christ.

(*He looks back at* DORIS *and then quickly moves to the dresser where he grabs a bottle of Wildroot Cream Oil, massages it into his scalp and starts to comb his short, tousled hair.*
   While he is doing this DORIS *wakes up, sits up in bed, watches him. At this point in time she is slightly overweight with ordinary pretty looks and a friendly, unself-conscious, ingenuous manner that makes her immediately appealing despite the fact that at twenty-four she hasn't had the time or the education to find out who or what she is yet. When she speaks there is a forced gaiety to her voice*)

DORIS
Hey, that's a real sharp-looking outfit.

(*At the sound of her voice he turns around to look at her*)

GEORGE
Uh—hi.

(*They eye one another for a moment*)

DORIS
What time is it?

GEORGE
Uh—my watch is on the bedside table.

(*As she leans over to look at his watch, he makes a distracted attempt to clean up the room. This consists of picking up his trousers and his right shoe. He puts on his trousers during the following*)

DORIS

(*Puzzled*)

It says ten to eleven.

GEORGE
No, it's twenty-five after seven. It's always three hours and twenty-five minutes fast.

DORIS
Why?

GEORGE
When I got it back from being fixed at the watchmaker's it was set three hours and twenty-five minutes fast. I decided to keep it that way.

DORIS

(*Bewildered*)

Doesn't that mix you up?

GEORGE
No, I'm very quick with figures.

DORIS
But what about other people?

GEORGE

(*Agitated*)

Look, it's *my* watch!

DORIS
What are you so sore about?

(*He takes a deep breath*)

GEORGE

(*Grimly*)

Because we're in a lot of trouble.

DORIS
Yeah?

GEORGE
God, why do you have to look so—so luminous!

DORIS
Luminous?

GEORGE
I mean it would make everything so much easier if you woke up with puffy eyes and blotchy skin like most women.

DORIS
I guess God figured chubby thighs was enough.

GEORGE
Look, this thing is not just going to go away. We've got to talk about it.

DORIS
Okay.

(*She gets out of bed, pulls the sheet out, puts it around her over her slip and heads across the room*)

GEORGE
What are you doing?

DORIS
I thought I'd clean my teeth first.

GEORGE
Dorothy, sit down.

(*She opens her mouth to speak*)

Please—sit.

(She moves to a chair, sits with the sheet wrapped around her.

He paces for a moment, gathering his thoughts before he turns to face her. When he speaks it is with great sincerity)

Dorothy, first of all, I want you to know last night was the most beautiful, fantastic, wonderful, crazy thing that's ever happened to me and I'll never forget it—or you.

DORIS
Doris.

GEORGE
What?

DORIS
My name's Doris.

GEORGE

(Thrown)

Why didn't you say so earlier? All last night I called you Dorothy and you never said anything.

DORIS
I didn't expect us to end up this—you know—

(She trails off)

Then when I did try to tell you—you weren't listening.

GEORGE
When?

DORIS
(*Embarrassed*)

It was—you know—in the middle of—things.

(*He fixes her with a look of smoldering intensity*)

GEORGE
It was incredible, wasn't it?

DORIS
It was—nice.

(*Sensing he expects something more*)

Especially the last time.

GEORGE

(*Anguished*)

I know—I'm an animal!

(*He throws the shoe he is holding into the sofa, moves away to look out of the window.*
   She takes this opportunity to kneel down to gather up some of her clothes)

I don't know what got into me. I just—what was the matter with the other two times?

DORIS
What? Oh—well, the first time was so fast and the second—look, I feel funny talking about this.

GEORGE

(*Earnestly*)

It was a very beautiful thing, Doris. There was nothing disgusting or dirty in what we did.

DORIS
Then how come you're looking so down in the dumps?

GEORGE
Because my wife is going to *kill* me!!

DORIS
Why should she find out?

GEORGE
She knows already.

DORIS
You said she was in New Jersey!

GEORGE

(*Gloomily*)

It doesn't matter. She *knows*.

DORIS
How come?

GEORGE
Look, I don't want to talk about it!

(*He stares at her*)

Doris, was it as incredible for you as it was for me?

DORIS

(*Curiously*)

Do all men like to talk about it a lot afterwards?

GEORGE

(*Defensively*)

Why? You think I'm some sort of—of eccentric or something?

DORIS
No, I just wondered. See, I was a virgin when I got married. At least technically.

GEORGE
Technically?

DORIS
Well, I was pregnant. I don't count that.

GEORGE

(*Doubtfully*)

Doris, that counts.

DORIS
I mean it was by the man I married.

GEORGE
Oh, I'm sorry.

(*She sits, puts on stocking during following*)

DORIS
That's okay. Harry and me would've got married anyway.
It just hurried things up a bit.

(*Brightly*)

Turns out I get pregnant if we drink from the same cup.

(*He looks at her, pales a little, and gulps*)

What's the matter?

GEORGE

(*Quickly*)

It's okay. Trojans are very reliable.

DORIS
Who are?

GEORGE
Never mind.

(*He stares at her*)

We're in a lot of trouble, Doris.

DORIS
Why?

GEORGE
I think I love you.

DORIS
Better not start up something we can't finish, George.

GEORGE
Maybe it's too late for that.

(*Suddenly*)

It's crazy! It's really crazy! I mean I don't even know if you like *Catcher in the Rye!*

DORIS
What?

GEORGE
I have this test for people. If they don't like *Catcher in the Rye* or *Death of a Salesman* I won't even date them!

DORIS
I never even finished high school.

GEORGE

(*Wildly*)

You see? I don't even *care!* And I'm really a *snob* about education!

(*He moves and bleakly stares out of window.* DORIS *puts on her skirt and blouse during the following*)

Of course I should've known this would happen. You see, there's something I didn't tell you about me, Doris.

DORIS
What?

GEORGE
When it comes to life I have a brown thumb. I mean nothing goes right. Ever.

DORIS
How do you mean?

GEORGE
Well, let me think of something that will give you the picture.

(*He thinks*)

Okay. I was eighteen when I first had sex. It was in the back seat of a parked 1938 Dodge sedan. Right in the middle of it—we were rear ended.

DORIS
Gee, that's terrible. Did you have insurance?

GEORGE
And take last night. You know what they were playing on the juke box when we met?

(*She shakes her head*)

"If I Knew You Were Coming I'd've Baked a Cake"!

DORIS

(*Puzzled*)

So?

GEORGE
So that's going to be "our song"!

(*He moves to angrily throw a log on the smoldering fire*)

Other people would get "Be My Love" or "Hello, Young Lovers." Me—I get "If I Knew You Were Coming I'd've Baked a Cake"!

DORIS

(*Sentimentally*)

You're very romantic. I like that.

(*He looks at her*)

GEORGE
And what about you? I think I've fallen in love with you, Doris. Now you want to know the luck I have? I'm happily married!

DORIS

(*Curiously*)

Are you Jewish?

GEORGE

(Thrown)

No, I'm not Jewish.

(He takes off coat, puts on shirt)

As a matter of fact, I'm the result of a very strict Methodist upbringing.

DORIS
Is that why you feel so guilty?

GEORGE
Don't *you* feel guilty?

DORIS
Are you kidding? Half my high school graduating class became nuns.

GEORGE
Yeah, I guess Catholics have rules about this sort of thing.

DORIS
They have rules about everything. That's what's so great about being Catholic. You know where you stand and all.

(He looks at her for a moment, shakes his head, starts to pace)

GEORGE
I tell you, Doris, I feel like slitting my wrists.

DORIS
Are you Italian?

GEORGE
What's with you and nationalities?

DORIS
You're so emotional.

GEORGE
I happen to be a C.P.A. I mean I can be as logical as the next person.

DORIS
You don't strike me as an accountant type.

GEORGE
It's very simple.

(*He shrugs*)

My whole life has always been a mess. Figures always come out right. Black and white, nice and tidy. I like that. What are you?

DORIS
Italian.

GEORGE

(*Thrown*)

Then why aren't you more emotional?

(*She moves to fire and warms her hands*)

DORIS

If you're brought up in a large Italian family it's enough to turn you off emotion for life, you know?

GEORGE

I wondered why you weren't crying or yelling or anything.

DORIS

I got up this morning and did all that in the john.

GEORGE

Crying?

DORIS

Yelling.

GEORGE

I didn't hear you.

DORIS

I put a towel in my mouth.

GEORGE

Oh, I'm sorry.

DORIS

That's okay. There's no use crying over spilt milk.

GEORGE

You're right.

DORIS

Then why are we feeling so lousy?

GEORGE

(*Soberly*)

Because we're both decent, honest people and this thing is tearing us apart. I mean I know it wasn't our fault but I keep seeing the faces of my children and the look of betrayal in their eyes. I keep thinking of the trust my wife has placed in me. The times we've shared together. Our wedding vows. And you know the worst part of it all? Right at this moment, while I'm thinking all these things I have this fantastic hard on!

(*She looks at him for a moment, not moving*)

DORIS

(*Finally*)

I wish you hadn't said that.

GEORGE
I'm sorry. I just feel we should be totally honest with each other.

DORIS
No, it's not that. I have to go to confession.

(*He looks at her for a second, breaks into rather a forced, incredulous laugh, moves away, turns to her, chuckles*)

GEORGE
This is really very funny, you know that?

DORIS
Tell me—I could use a good laugh.

GEORGE
We're both crazy! I mean this sort of thing happens to millions of people every day. We're just normal, healthy human beings who did a perfectly healthy, normal thing. You don't use actual names in confession, do you?

DORIS
No.

GEORGE
Good. You want to know what I think about marriage and sex?

DORIS
I don't want to miss confession, George.

GEORGE
After you've heard what I have to say maybe you won't need to even go.

(*He moves and sits cross-legged before her*)

Look, suppose you compare a husband or a wife to a good book. So you got this great book and you read it—it's terrific; you love it. So you read the book again. Still good. So you read it again and again and again and even after maybe a hundred times you still enjoy it. Well, you know the book by heart now, so for a little variety you read it standing up, then lying down, then upside down, backwards, sideways, every way you can think of. You still like it, but Jesus, how many ways are there to read a book?

Just once in a while you want to hear a new story, right? It doesn't mean you *hate* the old book. You'll read it again—later. Who knows? Maybe you'll appreciate it more.

(*A beat*)

You understand what I'm saying?

DORIS
There's no use crying over spilt milk?

GEORGE

(*Getting to his feet*)

Doris, you've missed the whole point!

DORIS
What is the point?

GEORGE

(*Intensely*)

I've got to go to bed with you right now!

(*He embraces her passionately and starts to smother her with kisses*)

DORIS
George, we can't!

GEORGE
Why not?

DORIS
You'll feel even worse afterwards!

GEORGE

(*Still kissing her*)

I won't, I won't! I'm over that now!

DORIS
How come?

GEORGE
I just remembered something!

DORIS
What?

GEORGE
The Russians have the bomb! We could all die tomorrow!

DORIS

(*Somewhat out of breath*)

George—you're clutching at straws!

(*He grabs her by the shoulders, looks deep into her eyes*)

GEORGE
Don't you understand? We're both grown-up people who have absolutely nothing to be ashamed or afraid of!!!

(*There is a knock at the door. Both freeze, their eyes reflecting total panic. Then they go into frantic action as*

*they both dive for the clothes on the floor. He gets her
girdle but is not aware of what is in his hand. She,
clutching the sheet and her shoes, bumps into him as she
first tries to get under the bed and then heads for the
bathroom door)*

GEORGE

(Panic-stricken—in a desperate hiss)

Don't go into the bathroom!

(She freezes)

DORIS
Why not?

GEORGE
It's the first place they'll look!

*(She heads for the window and climbs out onto the
balcony as he frantically tries to make the room
presentable.*

    *He looks around, sees she has disappeared but doesn't
know where as he heads for the door)*

I'm coming!

*(He opens the door about six inches and squeezes
outside, closing the door behind him.*

    *We hear a muffled exchange offstage before the door
reopens and he reenters pushing a cart containing
breakfast)*

Doris?

(She doesn't appear and, puzzled, he looks under the bed, then in the closet, then moves to the window, pushes it open and leans outside)

Doris?

(While he is doing this she comes back into the room through the other window, moves to behind him, claps a firm hand on his shoulder, speaks in a deep voice)

DORIS
You have a woman in here?

(He leaps about a foot in the air with a yelp, turns to face her. She giggles and finally he gives a sheepish grin)

GEORGE
It's okay, it was old Mr. Chalmers with my breakfast. I was very calm. He didn't suspect a thing.

DORIS
He didn't ask about the girdle?

GEORGE
What girdle?

(He looks in his hand, sees he is still clutching her girdle. Anguished)

Oh—great! Now he probably thinks I'm a—a homo!

DORIS
What do you care?

GEORGE
I stay here every year.

(*She moves to peek under platters on breakfast cart*)

DORIS
How come?

GEORGE
There's this guy I went to school with who went into the
wine business near here. I fly out the same weekend every
year to do his books.

DORIS
From New Jersey?

GEORGE
He was my first client. It's kind of a sentimental thing.

DORIS
Oh.

(*She looks at him*)

Uh—can I have my girdle back?

GEORGE
Oh, sorry—sure.

(*He extends girdle, she reaches for it but he keeps hold
of the other end, so they are both holding an end*)

Doris, there's something I want to tell you.

DORIS
What?

GEORGE
You probably think I do this sort of thing all the time. I mean I know I must appear smooth and glib—sexually. Well, I want you to know that since I've been married this is the very first time I've done this.

   (*A beat*)

Do you believe me?

DORIS
Sure, I could tell. Hey, you mind if I have some of your breakfast? I'm starved!

GEORGE
Oh sure—help yourself, I'm not hungry.

   (*She takes her girdle, pulls a chair up to the cart and starts to eat as he starts to pace*)

It's funny, even when I was single I was no good at quick, superficial affairs. I had to be able to really *like* the person before—

   (*Turning to her suddenly*)

What do you mean, you could tell?

DORIS

What? Oh—I don't know—the way you tried to get your pants off over your shoes and then tripped and hit your head on the bed post.

(Her eyes twinkling)

Little things like that.

(He smiles at her affectionately)

GEORGE
It's great to be able to be totally honest with another person, isn't it?

DORIS
It sure is.

(His expression changes)

GEORGE
Doris, I haven't been totally honest with you.

DORIS
No?

GEORGE
No.

(He takes a deep breath)

Okay—here it comes—the big one.

(*She waits expectantly*)

I told you I was a married man with two children.

DORIS
You're not?

GEORGE
No. I'm a married man with *three* children.

DORIS
I don't get it.

GEORGE
I thought it would make me seem less married.

(*Under her gaze he becomes agitated and starts to pace*)

Look, I just didn't think it through. Anyway, it's been like a lead weight inside me all morning. I mean denying little Debbie like that. I'm sorry, I was under a certain stress or I wouldn't have done it. You understand?

DORIS
Sure, we all do nutty things sometimes.

(*He smiles in relief*)

So how come your wife doesn't travel with you?

GEORGE
Phyllis won't get on a plane.

DORIS
She's afraid of flying?

GEORGE
Crashing.

(*He watches her eat for a moment. She looks up*)

DORIS
What's the matter?

GEORGE
Nothing. I just love the way you eat.

(*She grins at him, holds up coffee pot*)

DORIS
You wanta share a cup of coffee?

(*He nods, pulls up a chair opposite her, gazes at her as she pours coffee*)

GEORGE
Doris, I've been thinking. Sometimes if you *know* why something happened it makes it easier to understand.

DORIS
You mean like us?

GEORGE
Right. Doris, do you believe that two total strangers can look across a room and both have this sudden, overwhelming, totally irrational desire to possess one another in every possible way?

(*She considers for a moment*)

DORIS
No.

GEORGE

(*Puzzled*)

Neither do I—so I guess that can't be it. Then how did this whole thing start?

DORIS

It started when you sent me over that steak in the restaurant.

GEORGE

They didn't serve drinks. Steak was all they had.

DORIS

What made you do it?

GEORGE

Impulse. Usually I never do that sort of thing. I have this—this friend who says that life is saying "yes."

(*He shrugs*)

The most I can generally manage is "maybe."

DORIS

Your wife sounds like a nice person.

(*He reacts*)

So why'd you do it?

GEORGE

I guess I was lonely and you looked so—so vulnerable and—well, you had a run in your stocking and your lipstick was smeared.

DORIS
You thought I looked cheap?

GEORGE

(*Quickly*)

No—beautiful. I'm attracted by flaws. I don't know—
somehow they make people seem more human and—
approachable.

(*She gazes at him affectionately*)

That's why I like Pete Reiser better than say—Joe
DiMaggio.

DORIS
Pete Reiser's a baseball player?

GEORGE
He keeps running into walls. I like that.

DORIS

(*Gently*)

You know something, George? You're a real nice guy.

(*They smile tenderly at one another*)

What made you think I was a medium rare?

GEORGE
I'm very intuitive.

DORIS
I'm well-done.

(*This jolts George out of his romantic mood*)

GEORGE
Well-done? How can anyone like meat well-done?

DORIS
Harry always has his that way.

GEORGE
Oh. What were you doing in the restaurant anyway?

DORIS
I was on my way to a retreat. I go this same weekend every year.

GEORGE

(*Thrown*)

To—uh—meditate?

DORIS
Yeah, you might call it that. But not about God or anything. More about—well—myself.

(*He waits, awkwardly*)

See, I got pregnant when I was just eighteen and so I never had a chance to—well—live it up. Oh, I don't know what I'm trying to say.

(She shakes her head, gives a little laugh)

Sometimes I think I'm crazy.

GEORGE
Why?

DORIS

(Awkwardly, thinking it out)

Well, look at my life. I got three little kids underfoot all the time, so I'm never alone. I live in a two-bedroom duplex in downtown Oakland, we got a 1948 Kaiser that's almost half paid for, a blond three-piece dinette set, a Motorola TV, and we go bowling at least once a week.

(A beat)

I mean, what else could anyone ask for? But sometimes things get me down, you know? It's dumb!

GEORGE
I don't think it's dumb.

DORIS
I don't know. Sometimes I—I don't know what I *think* about anything, you know? I mean I'm almost twenty-five and I still feel—well—half-formed.

(He doesn't say anything.
A look of wonder comes to her face)

Will you listen to me? Honest, you make me say things out loud I haven't even *thought* to myself.

(She smiles at him)

I noticed that right after I met you last night.

GEORGE

(Eagerly)

We had instant rapport! Did you notice that too?

DORIS
No, but I know we really hit it off.

(A beat)

You want some more coffee?

(He shakes his head and watches her as she rises, moves to get sheet from where it was stuffed under the sofa, takes it to bed and starts to make bed)

GEORGE
What happens to your kids when you go on your retreat?

DORIS
Oh, Harry takes them to see his mother in Bakersfield. It's her birthday.

GEORGE
She doesn't mind you not going?

DORIS
No, she hates me.

GEORGE
Why?

DORIS
Because I got pregnant.

   (*He moves to help her make up bed*)

GEORGE
But her son had something to do with that too.

DORIS
She's blocked that out of her mind. Oh, I don't blame her.
You see, Harry was in first year of dental college.

GEORGE
I don't get the connection.

DORIS
He had to drop out of school and take a job selling
waterless cooking.

GEORGE
Oh.

   (*He moves away, watches her make up bed for a
   moment*)

Look, Doris, naturally we're both curious about each
other's husband and wife. But rather than dwelling on
it and letting it spoil everything, why don't we do this?
I'll tell you two stories—one showing the best side of
my wife and the other showing the worst. Then you
do the same about your husband. Okay?

DORIS
Okay.

GEORGE
I think I should go first.

DORIS
Why?

GEORGE
Because I already have my stories prepared.

(She nods, sits cross-legged on bed)

I'll start with the worst side of her.

DORIS
Go ahead.

GEORGE

(Grimly)

Phyllis knows about us.

DORIS
You said that before. How could she possibly know?

GEORGE
Because she has this—thing in her head.

DORIS
You mean like a plate?

GEORGE

(*Thrown*)

Plate?

DORIS
I got this uncle who was wounded in the war so they put this steel plate in his head and he says he can tell when it's going to rain.

(*He looks at her for a moment*)

GEORGE
Jesus, I'm in a lot of trouble.

DORIS
Why?

GEORGE
Because I find everything you say absolutely *fascinating!*

DORIS
Tell me about your wife's steel plate.

GEORGE
What?

(*Brought back to earth, miserably*)

No, it's not a plate—it's more like a bell.

(*Becoming agitated*)

I could be a million miles away but whenever I even *look* at another woman it goes off like a fire alarm! Last night at 1:22. I just know she sat bolt upright in bed with her head going, ding, ding, ding, ding!

(*He nervously moves to breakfast cart and absently starts wiping off the lipstick marks on the coffee cup with his handkerchief*)

DORIS
How'd you know it was 1:22?

GEORGE
I have peripheral vision and I noticed my watch said 4:47.

DORIS
That's crazy.

GEORGE
Okay, I happen to have personal idiosyncrasies and I happen to like my watch to be—

DORIS
No, I didn't mean that. I mean about your wife's bell and all.

GEORGE
Look, I know it's just an imaginary bell but it's very real to me!

(*He throws his lipstick-smeared handkerchief into the fire*)

DORIS

(*Incredulous*)

You just threw your hankie into the fire.

GEORGE
We can't be too careful.

DORIS
Tell me something nice about her.

GEORGE
What? Oh—she made me believe in myself.

(*He looks at her. Seriously*)

It's probably hard for you to imagine, but I used to be **very** insecure.

DORIS
How did she do that? Make you believe in yourself?

GEORGE
She married me.

DORIS
Yes, that was very nice of her.

(*He looks at her*)

I mean bolstering you up and all.

(*He lies on the couch*)

GEORGE
Okay, your turn. Tell me the worst story first.

DORIS
Well—it's hard—

GEORGE

(*Eagerly*)

To pick one?

DORIS
No, to think of one. Harry's the salt of the earth—everyone says so.

(*He sits upright*)

GEORGE
Look, you owe me one rotten story.

DORIS
Okay. This is not really rotten but—well—

(*She gets off the bed, moves to fire, looks into it for a moment*)

On our fourth anniversary we were having kind of a rough time. The kids were getting us down and—well, we'd gotten in over our heads financially but we decided to have some friends over anyway.

(*She moves to look out of window*)

Now Harry doesn't drink much, but that night he had a few beers and after the Gillette fights he and some of the guys started to talk and I overheard him say his time in the Army were the best years of his life.

GEORGE

(*Puzzled*)

What's wrong with that? A lot of guys feel that way about the service.

(*She turns to face him*)

DORIS
Harry was in the Army four years. Three of those years were spent in a Japanese prison camp!

(*A beat*)

And he said this on our anniversary! Oh, I know he didn't mean to hurt me—Harry would never hurt anyone—but, well, it—hurt, you know?

(*A beat*)

You're the only person I've ever told.

GEORGE
You want some more coffee?

DORIS
I'll get lipstick on the cup.

GEORGE
I don't care.

(*He moves to pour her coffee*)

DORIS
You wanta hear a story about the good side of him?

GEORGE
Not really.

DORIS
But you have to! I mean, I don't want you to get the wrong impression about Harry.

GEORGE
Okay, if you insist.

(*She moves to bed, plumps pillows*)

DORIS
Well, Harry's a real big, kind of heavyset sort of guy, you know?

GEORGE
I wish you hadn't told me that.

DORIS
Oh, you don't have to worry. He's gentle as—as a puppy.

(*She sits on the downstage side of the bed, facing front and clasps a pillow to her chest*)

Anyway, he tries to do different things with each of the kids, you know?

(*He sits beside her on the bed, hands her coffee*)

Thanks. So, he was having a hard time finding something special to do with Tony, our four-year-old. Then he gets the idea to take him out to the park and fly this big kite. Well, he tells Tony about it—really builds it up—and Tony gets real excited. So this one Saturday last winter they go out together, but there's no wind and Harry has trouble getting the kite to take off. Well, it's kind of cold and Tony, who's pretty bored by now—he's only four years old—asks if he can sit in the car. Harry says, "Sure."

(*She starts to smile*)

About an hour later I happen to come by on my way home from the laundromat and I see Tony fast asleep in the car and Harry, all red in the face and out of breath, pounding up and down, all alone in the park, with this kite dragging along behind him on the ground.

(*Her smile fades*)

I don't know—somehow it really got to me.

(*He looks at her, touched more by her reaction than by the story itself*)

GEORGE
Yeah, I know. Helen has some nice qualities too.

DORIS
Who's Helen?

GEORGE

(*Puzzled*)

My wife of course.

DORIS
You said her name was Phyllis.

(*Caught—a split moment of panic*)

GEORGE
I know—I lied.

(*She stares at him bewildered. Agitated*)

Helen—Phyllis—what's the difference? I'm married!

(*He gets up, paces*)

Look, I was nervous and I didn't want to leave any *clues!* I
mean I was scared you'd try to look me up or something!

DORIS
Is your real name George?

GEORGE
Of course it is! You don't think I'd lie about my own name
do you?

DORIS

(*Baffled*)

You're crazy.

GEORGE
Well, I never claimed to be consistent!

DORIS

(*Gently*)

Crazy.

(*She holds out the coffee cup to him, their hands touch and they become aware of the contact.*
Their eyes meet. He sits beside her)

GEORGE

(*Tenderly*)

It's funny, isn't it? Here we are having breakfast in a hotel room, gazing into each other's eyes, and we're both married with six kids between us.

DORIS
You got pictures?

GEORGE

(*Thrown*)

What?

DORIS
Pictures of your kids.

GEORGE

  (*Uncomfortably*)

Well, sure, but I don't think this is the time or place to—

  (*She moves for her purse*)

DORIS
I'll show you mine if you show me yours.

  (*Getting snapshots from purse*)

I keep them in a special folder we got free from Kodak.

  (*She returns to bed, hands him snaps*)

Where are yours?

GEORGE

  (*Still off-balance*)

Uh—you have to take the whole wallet.

  (*He extracts wallet from his back pocket, hands it to her.
     They are now seated side by side on the bed, looking
  at each other's snapshots*)

DORIS
Oh, they're cute! Is the one in the glasses and baggy tights
the oldest?

GEORGE

(*Looking at snap*)

Yes, that's Michael. Funny-looking kid isn't he?

DORIS
He wants to be Superman?

GEORGE
Peter Pan. Sometimes it worries me.

(*Looking at snaps in his hand*)

Why is this one's face all screwed up?

DORIS
Oh, that's Paul—it was taken on a roller coaster. Isn't it natural? He threw up right after that.

GEORGE
Yeah, he's really—something. I guess he looks like Harry, huh?

DORIS
Both of us really.

(*Looking at snap*)

What's your little girl's name?

GEORGE
Debbie. That was taken on her second birthday. We were trying to get her to blow out the candles.

DORIS
She has her hand in the cake.

GEORGE
Yeah, neat is not her strong suit.

   (*They look at one another*)

DORIS
You have great-looking kids, George.

GEORGE
You too.

DORIS
Thanks.

   (*There is a slight pause*)

GEORGE
Doris?

DORIS
Yeah?

GEORGE
Let's dump the lot of them and run away together!

   (*She looks at him astonished, and the lights fade for the—*)

END OF ACT I, SCENE 1

SCENE 2

THE TIME:
A day in February, 1956.

THE PLACE:
The same.

AT RISE:
GEORGE, wearing a charcoal suit and pink shirt of the period, has just hung a home-made sign reading "HAPPY FIFTH ANNIVERSARY, DARLING" on the front door. He has put on a few pounds, his hair has just started to thin, and at thirty-two he gives the impression of more substance. It is just an impression. Although his manner is more subdued than five years ago and his insecurities flash through less frequently, it is only because he has learned a degree of control of his mercurial moods. He takes a small birthday cake from a box and places it beside two plates and forks on the coffee table.

DORIS

(*Offstage*)

Damn!

GEORGE
What's the matter?

DORIS

(*Offstage*)

It's my merry widow.

GEORGE
Your what?

DORIS

(*Offstage*)

Merry widow. It mashes you in and pushes you out in all
the right places. It also gives you this pale, wan look
because it cuts off all circulation.

GEORGE
Be sure and let me know when you're coming out.

DORIS

(*Offstage*)

Right now.

GEORGE
Wait a minute!

(*He quickly moves to the piano, sits*)

Okay—now!

(As she enters he sings and plays "If I knew You Were Coming I'd Have Baked a Cake."

She is dressed in a strapless, black cocktail dress that was considered chic in the suburbs in the fifties; is slimmer than before and more carefully put together. The most striking physical change in her is her very blond hair, shaped in a Gina Lollobrigida cut. She has acquired some of the social graces of middle-class suburbia, is more articulate than before, and has developed a wry, deprecating wit that doesn't hide a certain terseness of manner.

He stops playing, moves to her and embraces her)

GEORGE
Happy anniversary, darling.

(He hands her a glass of champagne, they toast, drink, and he indicates the cake)

Cut the cake and make a wish.

(They move to sit on the sofa and he watches her as she cuts the cake)

What did you wish?

DORIS
I only have one wish.

GEORGE
What?

DORIS
That you keep showing up every year.

(*They kiss*)

GEORGE
I'm always surprised that you do. I was really surprised the second year.

(*He crosses to the piano and refills their glasses with champagne. He gives one to* DORIS)

Of course I had less confidence in my personal magnetism then. You know that was one of the best ideas you ever had?

DORIS
Meeting here every year?

GEORGE
No, refusing to run off with me. Weren't you even tempted?

DORIS
Sure I was. I still am. But I had the feeling that if we had run off together we'd end up with—well—with pretty much the same sort of nice, comfortable marriage we both already had at home.

(*They sit and drink*)

GEORGE
How are things at home?

DORIS

We moved to the suburbs. Right now everyone's very excited. Next week they're going to connect the sewers. Well it's not exactly the life of Scot and Zelda, but we'll survive.

GEORGE

(*Surprised*)

You started reading!

DORIS

Oh, you don't know the half of it. I joined the Book-of-the-Month Club.

GEORGE

Good for you.

DORIS

(*Kidding herself*)

Listen, sometimes I even take the *alternate* selections.

GEORGE

(*Sincerely*)

I'm really proud of you, honey.

DORIS

Well, it was either that or group mambo lessons. You still live in New Jersey?

GEORGE
No, we moved to Connecticut. We bought an old barn and
converted it.

DORIS
What's it like?

GEORGE
Drafty. Helen's got the decorating bug. At my funeral just
as they're closing the lid on my coffin I have this mental
picture of Helen throwing in two fabric swatches and
yelling, "Which one do you like?" That's the bad story
about her.

DORIS
What else is new?

GEORGE
We had a baby girl.

DORIS
Oh, George, that's marvelous! You have pictures?

GEORGE

  (*Grins*)

I knew you'd ask that.

  (*He takes out pictures, hands them to her*)

DORIS

  (*Looking at snaps*)

Oh, she's adorable. It's funny. I still like to look at new babies but I don't want to *own* one anymore. You think that's a sign of maturity?

GEORGE
Could be.

(*He takes out cigar*)

Here, I even kept one of these for you to give to Harry. It's from Havana.

DORIS
Harry still thinks I go on retreat. What should I tell him? It came from a Cuban nun?

(*She takes the cigar, moves to put it in her purse*)

So how are the rest of the kids? How's Michael?

GEORGE
Oh, crazy as ever. He had this homework assignment, to write what he did on his summer vacation. Trouble is, he chose to write what he actually did.

DORIS
What was that?

GEORGE
Tried to get laid. He wrote in great comic detail about his unfortunate tendency to get an erection on all forms of public transportation. The school almost suspended him.

DORIS
You're crazy about him, aren't you?

GEORGE
He's a very weird kid, Doris.

DORIS
And he really gets to you. Come on—admit it.

GEORGE
Okay, I admit it. He's a nice kid.

DORIS
See? Was that so hard?

(*He looks at her for a moment, crosses to her,
impulsively kisses her*)

DORIS
What was that for?

GEORGE
Everything. This. One beautiful weekend every year with
no cares, no ties and no responsibilities. Thank you,
Doris.

(*He kisses her again. The embrace grows more
passionate. They break*)

DORIS

(*Breathlessly*)

Gee, I just got all dressed up.

> (*They sink onto the bed. He is lying half on top of her
> when the phone rings*)

DORIS
Someone has a rotten sense of timing.

GEORGE
Let it ring. It's probably only Pete wanting to know how
much he owes the I.R.S.

DORIS
Chalmers probably told him we're in.

GEORGE
Damn.

> (*Without changing his position he reaches out and takes
> the phone*)

Hello.

> (*His expression changes—slowly but drastically*)

Is there anything wrong? Yes, this is Daddy—Funny?

> (*He slowly rolls off* DORIS *to a tense position on the edge
> of the bed*)

Well, that's probably because Daddy was just—uh—I had
a frog in my throat, sweetheart.

It came out huh? Which one was it?

(*He sits with the phone in his hand, bent over, almost as if he has a stomachache*)

Of course, the tooth-fairy will come, sweetheart—Why tonight, of course—It doesn't matter if you can't find it, darling, the tooth-fairy will know—Well, I wish I could be there to find it for you too, honey, but Daddy's working—Oh, in my room.

(*At this point* DORIS *gets off the bed and unobtrusively starts to clean up the room*)

Yes, it's a very nice room—Well, it has a fireplace and a sofa and a big comfortable b—

(*He can't bring himself to say "bed"*)

—bathroom. Well I'd like you to come with me too, sweetheart. Maybe next year—I'm afraid not, sweetheart. You see Daddy has to finish up his—business—well, I'll try—Yes, I love you too, honey—Yes, very much.

(*He hangs up and puts his head in his hands.*
    DORIS *crosses to him and wordlessly puts a comforting hand on his shoulder*)

Oh, God, I feel so *guilty!*

(*He rises and moves away*)

DORIS
Debbie?

GEORGE

Her tooth came out. She can't find it and she's worried the tooth-fairy won't know! Oh, God, that thin, reedy little voice. Do you know what that *does* to me!

DORIS

Sure, that calm exterior doesn't fool me for a minute.

GEORGE

You think this is *funny?*

DORIS

Honey, I understand how you feel but I really don't think it's going to help going on and on about it.

GEORGE

Doris, my little girl said, "I love you, Daddy," and I answered her with a voice still *hoarse with passion!*

DORIS

I think I've got the picture, George.

GEORGE

Don't you ever feel guilty?

DORIS

Sometimes.

GEORGE

You've never said anything.

DORIS

I just deal with it in a different way.

GEORGE
How?

DORIS
Privately.

(*Agitated,* GEORGE *starts pacing around the room*)

GEORGE
I don't know, maybe men are more—sensitive than women.

DORIS
Have a drink, George.

GEORGE
Perhaps women are more pragmatic than men.

DORIS
What's that mean?

GEORGE
They adjust to rottenness quicker. I mean, they're more inclined to live for the moment.

(*Offhandedly*)

Anyway, you have the church.

DORIS
The church?

GEORGE
Well, you're Catholic, aren't you? You can get rid of all your guilt at one sitting. I have to *live* with mine.

DORIS
I think *I'll* have a drink.

(*She moves to pour herself a drink*)

GEORGE
Boy, something like that really brings you up short!

(*Holding out his trembling hands*)

I mean *look* at me! I tell you, Doris—when she started talking about the tooth-fairy—well, it affected me in a very profound manner.

(*A beat*)

On top of that I have indigestion you can't *believe*. It hit me that hard, you know?

DORIS
George, I have three children too.

GEORGE
Sure, sure—I know. I don't mean that you don't *understand*. It's just that we're different people and your guilt is less—acute.

DORIS
Honey, what do you want to do? Have a guilt contest? Is that going to solve anything?

GEORGE
What do you want me to do, Doris?

DORIS
I think it might be a terrific idea if you stopped talking
about it. It's only making you feel worse.

GEORGE
I can't feel worse. That pure little voice saying—

(*He stops, tries to shake it off with a jerk of his head*)

No, you're right. Forget it.

(*Shakes his head again*)

Forget it. Talk about something else. Tell me about Harry.
Tell me the good story about Harry.

(*During the following,* GEORGE *tries to concentrate but is
obviously distracted and nervous*)

DORIS
Okay. He went bankrupt.

(*This momentarily jolts him out of his problem*)

GEORGE
How can anyone go bankrupt selling TV sets?

DORIS
Harry has this one weakness as a salesman. It's a
compulsion to talk people out of things they can't afford.
He lacks the killer instinct.

(*Reflectively*)

It's one of the things I like best about him. Anyway, he went into real estate.

(GEORGE *is staring out of the window*)

Your turn.

GEORGE
What?

DORIS
Tell me your story about Helen.

GEORGE
I already did.

DORIS
You just told me the bad one. Why do you always tell that one first?

GEORGE
It's the one I look forward to telling the most.

DORIS
Tell me the nice story about her.

GEORGE
Oh.

(*Moving about the room*)

Well—Chris—that's our middle one—ran into a lawn

sprinkler and gashed his knee really badly. Helen drove
both of us to the hospital.

DORIS
Both of you?

GEORGE
I fainted.

DORIS
Oh.

GEORGE
The nice part was she never told anybody.

DORIS
You faint often?

GEORGE
Only in emergencies.

DORIS
Is it the sight of blood that—

GEORGE
Please, Doris! My stomach's squeamish enough already.
Maybe I will have that drink.

(*He moves to liquor, speaks overcasually*)

Oh, listen, something just occurred to me. Instead of my
leaving at the usual time tomorrow night would you mind
if I left a little earlier?

DORIS

(*Puzzled*)

When did you have in mind?

GEORGE

Well, there's a plane in half an hour.

(*She stares at him astounded*)

DORIS

You want to leave *twenty-three hours early?*

(*He moves to suitcase, starts to pack and continues through the following as she watches with unbelieving eyes*)

GEORGE

Look, I know how you feel—I really do—and I wouldn't even *suggest* it if you weren't a mother yourself and didn't understand the situation. I mean I wouldn't even *think* of it if this crisis hadn't come up. Oh, it's not just the tooth-fairy—she could have *swallowed* the tooth. I mean it could be lodged God knows where! Now I know this leaves you a bit—uh—at loose ends but there's no reason for you to leave too. The room's all paid up. Anyway, I'm probably doing you a favor. If I did stay I wouldn't be very good company. Uh—have you seen my hairbrush?

(*He looks around, sees it is beside her*)

Doris, would you hand me my hairbrush?

(Without a word, she picks it up and throws it at him with much more force than necessary. It sails past his head and crashes against the wall.

There is a pause)

I think I can explain that. You feel somewhat rejected and, believe me, I can understand that but I want you to know my leaving has nothing to do with *you and me!*

(She just stares at him)

Doris, this is an *emergency!* I have a *sick child* at home!

DORIS

(Exploding)

Oh, will you *stop* it! It's got nothing to do with the goddam tooth-fairy! You're consumed with guilt and the only way you can deal with it is by getting as far away from me as possible!

GEORGE
Okay, I feel guilty. Is that so strange?

(Intensely)

Doris, don't you understand? We're *cheating!* Once a year we lie to our families and sneak off to a hotel in California and commit adultery!

(Holding up his hand)

Not that I want to stop doing it! But yes, I feel guilt. I admit it.

DORIS

(*Incredulous*)

You *admit* it!? You take out ads! You probably stop
strangers in the street! It's a wonder you haven't hired a
sky writer! I'm amazed you haven't had your shorts
monogrammed with a scarlet 'A' as a conversation starter!
You think that by *talking* about it, by wringing your hands
and beating your breast it will somehow excuse what you're
doing? So you wander around like—like an open nerve
saying, "I'm cheating but look how *guilty* I feel so I must
really be a nice guy!" And to top it all, you have the
incredible arrogance to think you're the only one in the
world with a conscience! Well, that doesn't make you a
nice guy. You know what it makes you? A *horse's ass!*

(*There is a pause*)

GEORGE

(*Finally*)

You know something? I liked you better *before* you started
reading.

DORIS
That's not why you're leaving, George.

GEORGE
Doris, it's not the end of the world. I'm not leaving you
permanently.

(*Turning to finish packing*)

We'll see each other again next year.

(*He shuts suitcase, snaps locks*)

DORIS

(*Quietly—with finality*)

There's not going to be a next year, George.

(*He turns to face her*)

GEORGE
You don't mean that.

(*He suspects by her face that she does*)

I can't believe that! Just because I have to leave early one year you're willing to throw away a lifetime of weekends? How can you be so—so *casual?*

DORIS
I don't see any point in going on.

(*He starts to shake his head*)

GEORGE
Oh no. Don't do that to me, Doris.

(*He takes suitcase, moves to deposit it by the door during following*)

Don't try to manipulate me. I get enough of that at home.

(*Getting raincoat, putting it on*)

That's not what our relationship is about.

DORIS

(*Soberly*)

What is it about, George?

GEORGE
You don't *know?*

DORIS
Yes. But it seems to be completely different from how you think about us. That's why I think we should stop seeing each other.

GEORGE

(*Finally*)

My God, you really *are* serious.

DORIS
George, what's the point of going on if we're going to come to each other burdened down with guilt and remorse? What joy is there in that?

GEORGE

(*Frustrated—indicating door*)

Doris, I have a commitment there.

DORIS

(*Quietly*)

And you don't have a commitment here?

GEORGE

(*Bewildered*)

Here? I thought our only commitment was to show up every year.

DORIS
Nice and tidy, huh? Just two friendly sexual partners who meet once a year, touch and let go.

GEORGE
Okay—so maybe I was kidding myself. I'm human.

DORIS
Well, so am I.

GEORGE

(*Sincerely*)

But you're different. Stronger. You always seem able to—cope.

(*She moves away, looks into the fire. She speaks slowly, deliberately unemotional*)

DORIS
George, during the past year I picked up the phone and
started to call you five times. I couldn't seem to stop
thinking about you. You kept slopping over into my real
life and it scared hell out of me. More to the point I felt
guilty. So I decided to stop seeing you.

> (*He is shaken.*
> *She turns to face him*)

At first I wasn't going to show up at all but then I
thought I at least owed you an explanation. So I came.

> (*She turns away*)

When you walked in the door I knew I couldn't do it.
That despite the price it was all worth it.

> (*A pause*)

GEORGE

> (*Finally—anguished*)

Oh God, I feel so *guilty!!*

DORIS

> (*Quietly—flatly*)

I think you'd better leave, George.

> (*There is a pause*)

GEORGE
I love you, Doris.

(*A beat*)

I'm an idiot. I suspect I'm deeply neurotic, and I'm no bargain—but I do love you.

(*He moves to her, gently turns her to face him*)

Will you let me stay?

(*They embrace, break, and gaze at one another*)

Doris, what are we going to do?

(*She reaches out and takes his hand*)

DORIS
Touch and hold on very tight. Until tomorrow.

(*They embrace. The lights slowly fade and the curtain falls*)

END OF ACT I, SCENE 2

SCENE 3

THE TIME:
A day in February, 1961.

THE PLACE:
The same.

AT RISE:
GEORGE, still wearing his raincoat and hat, is talking on the phone. His unpacked suitcase is in the middle of the floor and it is apparent that he has just arrived. As he talks he takes off his raincoat and throws it on the bed.

GEORGE

(*Irritably—into phone*)

No of course I haven't left Helen. I'm on a business trip. I come out here every year—I am not running away from the problem!

(*Becoming more angry*)

Of course I know it's serious. I still don't think it's any reason to phone me long distance and—Look, frankly, I don't think this is any of your business and to be totally honest I resent—

(*He gives an exasperated sigh*)

Yes, I saw a doctor—He said it's no big deal, that every man has this problem at one time or another and—Look, if we *have* to discuss this you may as well learn to pronounce it correctly. It's impotence, not im*p*otence—

(*Incredulous*)

What do you mean, did I catch it in time? It's a slight reflex problem not a terminal illness!

(*Frustrated*)

It's not something you have to "nip in the bud." Look, how did you find out about this anyway?—Dropped a few hints? What *sort* of hints?—You asked her and she looked funny. Terrific.

(*Exasperated again*)

Yes, of course I'm trying to do something about it—I don't have to tell you that—Look, will you let me deal with this in my own way? I'm going to be okay—Soon—I just *know,* that's all.

(*Flaring*)

I just *feel* it, okay?—I'm seeing someone out here who's an expert.

(*His patience exhausted*)

Look, I don't think we should be even *discussing*
this!—I'm sorry, I'm going to hang up now.

(*Firmly*)

Goodbye, Mother!

(*He slams the receiver down, picks up his raincoat, looks
at bed, throws raincoat over chair, turns blankets and
sheets down, tosses hat into chair revealing that his
hairline has receded noticeably. He then crosses to his
suitcase, puts it on rack, opens it, extracts pajamas and
robe and exits to bathroom. There is a slight pause
before the front door opens and* DORIS *enters. She is
obviously very, very pregnant. Her hair is back to her
normal color and her face looks softer than before.
Perspiring slightly, she puts her case down*)

DORIS

(*Calling*)

George!

GEORGE

(*Offstage—from bathroom*)

Be right out, darling!

(DORIS, *holding her back, moves to look out of the
window. When* GEORGE, *now dressed in robe and*

*pajamas, enters from the bathroom her back is towards
him. He stops, smiles at her tenderly)*

How are you, lover?

*(She turns to face him, revealing her eight months
pregnant stomach. His smile fades and his expression
becomes frozen. He just stares, unable to speak)*

DORIS

(Finally)

I know. I've heard of middle-aged spread but this is
ridiculous.

GEORGE

(In a strangled voice)

My God, what have you done to yourself?

DORIS
Well, I can't take all the credit. It was a mutual effort.

(He continues to stare at her)

Honey, when you haven't seen an old friend for a year isn't
it customary to kiss them hello?

GEORGE

(Still stunned)

What? Oh, sure.

(He moves to her, gives her a rather perfunctory kiss)

DORIS
Are you okay? You look funny.

GEORGE

(Flaring—moving away)

Funny? I'm hysterical!

DORIS
What's that mean?

(He tries to regain control)

GEORGE
Well—naturally, I'm—surprised, okay?

DORIS
You're surprised. I insisted on visiting the dead rabbit's grave!

(Puzzled)

Why are you wearing your pajamas and robe in the afternoon?

GEORGE

(Irritably)

I'm rehearsing for a Noël Coward play! Why the hell do you think?

DORIS
Oh, I'm sorry, darling. I'm afraid all that dirty stuff is out. That is, unless you have a ladder handy.

GEORGE
Doris, do you mind? I'm in no mood for bad taste jokes!

DORIS
Oh, come on, honey—where's your sense of humor? Look at it this way—maybe it's nature's way of telling us to slow down.

(*He watches her as she moves to a chair and awkwardly negotiates herself into the seat. She kicks off her shoes, massages her feet, looks up to find him staring at her with a baleful expression*)

George, is there something on your mind?

(*He moves away to the window*)

GEORGE
Not anymore.

DORIS
Then why are you so jumpy?

(*He wheels to face her*)

GEORGE
You must be eight months pregnant!

DORIS
Why are you so shocked? I am married.

GEORGE
You think that excuses it?

DORIS
What exactly are you trying to say?

GEORGE
I just consider it damned—irresponsible!

DORIS

(*Amused*)

Well, I have to admit, it wasn't planned!

GEORGE

(*Frustrated*)

I mean coming here in—in that condition!

DORIS
Well, I'm sorry you're disappointed, darling, but we'll just
have to find some other way to—communicate.

GEORGE
Great! You have any ideas?

DORIS
We could talk.

GEORGE
Talk? Talk I can get at home!

DORIS

   (*Grinning*)

Well, sex *I* can get at home. And as you can see, that's not just talk.

GEORGE
What the hell is that supposed to mean?

DORIS

   (*Shrugs*)

Well, I've never had any cause to complain about Harry in that department.

GEORGE
Oh really? And what does that make me? Chopped liver?

   (*She has been watching him with a curious expression*)

DORIS
George, what is the *matter* with you?

GEORGE
Matter? I'm the only man in America who just kept an illicit assignation with a woman who—who looks like a—frigate in full sail! And you ask what's the matter?

DORIS

(*Calmly*)

No, there's something else. You're not yourself.

GEORGE
Let me be the judge of who I am, okay?

DORIS
Why are you so *angry?*

GEORGE
What was the crack about Harry? Is that supposed to reflect on me? You don't think I have normal desires and sex drives?

DORIS
Of course not. You're very normal. I just meant I look forward to seeing you for a lot of reasons *beside* sex. Do you think we would have lasted this long if that's all we had in common?

GEORGE

(*Grudgingly*)

No, I guess not.

DORIS
We're friends as well as lovers, aren't we?

GEORGE
Yes.

(He sighs)

I'm sorry, Doris. I've—I've had a lot on my mind lately and—well, seeing you like that took the wind out of my sails. You want a drink?

DORIS
No, you go ahead. Alcohol makes me go a funny shade of pink.

(She watches him as he moves to extract a bottle from his suitcase)

You want to tell me about it?

GEORGE
No, it's not something I can really *talk* about.

(He moves to get glass, pours drink, shrugs)

It's just I was looking forward to an—intimate weekend.

DORIS
You think we can only be intimate through sex?

GEORGE
I think it sure helps.

DORIS
Oh, maybe at the beginning.

GEORGE
The beginning?

DORIS
Well, every year we meet it's a bit strange and awkward at first but we usually solve that in between the sheets with a lot of heavy breathing.

GEORGE
Doris, if we're not going to do it, would you mind not talking about it?

DORIS
I just meant maybe we need something else to—break the ice.

GEORGE

(*Pouring himself another drink*)

I'm willing to try anything.

DORIS
How about this? Supposing I tell you something about myself I've never told anyone before in my life?

GEORGE
I think I've had enough surprises for one day.

DORIS
You'll like this one.

(*She gets out of the chair with some difficulty and moves to look out of window.*
He watches and waits)

I've been having these sex dreams about you.

GEORGE
When?

DORIS
Just lately. Almost every night.

GEORGE
What sort of dreams?

(*She turns to face him*)

DORIS
That's what's so strange. They're always the same. We're making love under water. In caves, grottos, swimming pools—but always under water. Isn't that weird?

(*She shrugs*)

Probably something to do with me being pregnant.

GEORGE
Under water, huh?

(*She nods*)

DORIS
Now you tell me some deep, dark secret about yourself.

GEORGE
I can't swim.

DORIS

(*Puzzled*)

Literally?

GEORGE

   (*Irritably*)

Of course literally! When I tell you I can't swim I
simply mean I can't swim!

DORIS
How come?

GEORGE
I just never learned when I was a kid. But I never told
anybody—well, Helen found out when she pushed me off a
dock and I almost drowned—but my kids don't even know.
When we go to the beach I pretend I'm having trouble with
my trick knee.

DORIS
You have a trick knee?

GEORGE
No. They don't know that either.

   (*She moves to him, puts her hand on his cheek*)

DORIS
You see, it worked.

   (*He looks puzzled*)

We're talking just like people who have been to bed and
everything.

(She moves to another chair, carefully lowers herself into it. The effort tires her)

Boy, I'll tell you—that Ethel Kennedy must really like kids.

GEORGE
Hey, I'm sorry about—earlier. I'm glad to see you anyway.

DORIS
You want to tell me what it was all about?

(He looks at her for a moment)

GEORGE
Okay, I may as well get it out in the open. I mean it's nothing to be ashamed about.

(He takes a turn around the room)

It's very simple really. It's my—sex life. Lately, Helen hasn't been able to satisfy me.

DORIS

(Surprised)

She's lost her interest in sex?

GEORGE
Oh, she tries—God knows. But I can tell she's just going through the motions.

DORIS
Do you have any idea why this is?

GEORGE
Well, Helen's always had a lot of hangups about sex. For
one thing she's always thought of it as just a healthy,
normal, pleasant function. Don't you think that's a bit
twisted?

DORIS
Only if you're Catholic.

GEORGE

(*Earnestly*)

You're joking but there's a lot to be said for guilt. I mean if
you don't feel guilty or ashamed about it I think you're
missing half the fun. To Helen—sex has always been good,
clean—*entertainment*. No wonder she grew tired of it.

(*He finds* DORIS' *gaze somewhat disconcerting*)

Look, I don't know, for some reason my sex drive has
increased while hers has decreased.

DORIS
That's odd. Usually, it's the other way around.

GEORGE

(*Defensively*)

Are you accusing me of lying?

DORIS
Of course not. Why are you so edgy?

GEORGE
Because—well, I don't think it's fair to talk about this behind her back when she's not here to defend herself.

(*She watches him as he moves to pour another drink*)

DORIS
Would you like to get to the more formal part of your presentation?

GEORGE
What? Oh—okay. I'll start with the nice story about her.

DORIS
You've never done that before. You must be mellowing.

GEORGE
Doris, do you mind? Where was I? Oh—yeah. We were checking into a hotel in London and there was a man in a morning coat and striped trousers standing at the front entrance. Helen handed him her suitcases and sailed on into the lobby. The man followed her in with her suitcases and very politely pointed out that not only didn't he work at the hotel but that he was the Danish Ambassador. Without batting an eye she said, "Well, that's marvelous. Maybe you can tell us the good places to eat in Copenhagen." And he did. The point is it doesn't bother her when she makes a total ass of herself. I really admire that.

DORIS
And what don't you admire?

GEORGE

It's that damned sense of humor of hers!

DORIS

Oh, those are the stories I like the best.

(He looks at her for a moment, then launches headlong into the story)

GEORGE

We'd come home from a party and we'd had a few drinks and we went to bed and we started to make love. Well, nothing happened—for me—I couldn't—well, you get the picture. It was no big deal—and we laughed about it. Then about half an hour later, just as I was dropping off to sleep she said, "It's funny, when I married a C.P.A. I always thought it would be his eyes that would go first."

DORIS

(Finally)

She was just trying to make you feel better, George.

GEORGE

Well, it didn't. Some things aren't funny.

(DORIS doesn't say anything)

I suppose what I'm trying to say is that the thing that bugs me most about Helen is that she broke my pecker!

DORIS

(Gently)

You're impotent?

GEORGE
Slightly.

(*He gives a shrug*)

Okay, now five people know. Me, you, Helen and her mother.

DORIS
Who's the fifth?

GEORGE
Chet Huntley. I'm sure her mother has given him the bulletin for the six o'clock news.

DORIS
I thought that might be it.

GEORGE
You mean you can tell just by *looking* at me?

DORIS

(*Sympathetically*)

When did it happen, honey?

GEORGE
Happen? Doris, we're not talking about a freeway accident! I mean you don't wake up one morning and say, "Oh shoot, the old family jewels have gone on the blink." It's a—a gradual thing.

DORIS
And you really blame Helen for this?

GEORGE
Of course not. I—I wanted to tell you but I just couldn't think of a graceful way of working it into the conversation.

(*He gives a short, hard laugh*)

To tell you the truth I was just waiting for you to say "What's new?" And I was going to say "Nothing, but I can tell you what's old."

DORIS
How's Helen reacting?

GEORGE
Oh, we haven't talked about it much but I get the feeling she regards it as a lapse in one's social responsibility. You know, rather like letting your partner down in tennis by not holding your serve.

(*He gives a little laugh*)

Look, it's not great tragedy. As they say in Brooklyn, "Just wait 'til next year."

(*She is not smiling*)

Seriously, I'll be okay. Send no flowers. The patient's not dead yet—just resting.

(*She extends her hand*)

Doris, that statement hardly calls for congratulations.

DORIS
I need help to get out of this chair.

(*He pulls her out of the chair*
   Takes his face between her hands. Simply)

I'm really sorry.

(*They look tenderly at one another for a moment before*
he suddenly jerks away)

GEORGE
What the hell was that?

DORIS
The baby kicking.

GEORGE

(*Moving away*)

Well, everyone else has taken a shot at me. Why not him?

DORIS

(*Puzzled*)

It's strange. He hasn't been kicking lately. Maybe he
resents the bumpy ride up here.

(*She sees that* GEORGE *is not really listening*)

Is there anything I can say that will help?

GEORGE
What? Honey, you can say anything you want except "It's all in your head." I mean I'm no doctor but I have a great sense of direction.

(*As she starts to talk*)

Look, to tell you the truth, I'm not too crazy about this whole discussion. Let's forget it, huh?

DORIS
Okay. What do you want to talk about?

GEORGE
Anything but sex. How'd you feel about being pregnant?

DORIS
Catatonic, incredulous, angry, pragmatic, and finally maternal. Pretty much in that order.

GEORGE
Your vocabulary's improving.

DORIS
Ah, you didn't know. You're talking to a high school graduate.

GEORGE

(*Puzzled*)

How come?

DORIS

Well, I was confined to bed for the first three months of my pregnancy, so rather than it being a total loss I took a correspondence course.

GEORGE

(*Admiringly*)

You're really something, you know that?

DORIS

There's kind of an ironic twist to all this.

GEORGE
Oh?

DORIS

Well, I didn't graduate the first time because I got pregnant. And now I did graduate because—

(*She grins, taps her stomach*)

Appeals to my sense of order.

GEORGE

(*Teasing*)

I didn't know you had a sense of order.

DORIS

That's unfair. I'm much better at housework lately. Now I'm only two years behind in my ironing. Must be the

nesting instinct. Anyway, the day my diploma came in the
mail Harry bought me a corsage and took me out dancing.
Well, we didn't really dance—we lumbered. Afterwards we
went to a malt shop and had a fudge sundae. That's the
nice story about him.

GEORGE
He still selling real estate?

DORIS
Insurance. He likes it. Gives him an excuse to look up all
his old Army buddies.

(*He regards her as she stands with her stomach thrust
out and both hands pressed on either side of her back*)

GEORGE
Doris, are you comfortable in that position?

DORIS
Honey, when you're in my condition you're not
comfortable in any position.

(*He takes her arm, leads her to a chair*)

GEORGE
Come on, sit over here.

(*He helps lower her into the chair. As he does a strange
expression comes to his face*)

DORIS
Thanks. How are the kids?

GEORGE

(*Vaguely*)

What? Oh, fine. Michael got a job with Associated Press.

DORIS

Oh, darling, that's marvelous. I'm so proud of him.

(*She notices that he is staring at her with an odd, fixed expression*)

George, why are you looking at me like that?

GEORGE

(*Too quickly*)

No reason. It—it's nothing.

DORIS

Does my stomach offend you?

GEORGE

No, it's not that. Tell me your other story about Harry.

DORIS

I had trouble telling him I was pregnant. When I finally did he looked at me for a moment and then said "Is there a revolver in the house?" George, you're doing it again! What *is* it?

GEORGE

(*Exploding*)

It's obscene!

DORIS

(*Bewildered*)

What is?

GEORGE

When I touched you I started to get excited!!!!

(*He paces around*)

What kind of pervert am I?

(*He turns to look at her*)

I'm staring at a two hundred pound woman and I'm getting hot! Just the *sight* of you is making me excited.

(*She looks at him for a moment*)

DORIS

(*Finally*)

Let me tell you something. That's the nicest thing anyone's said to me in months.

GEORGE

(*Very agitated*)

It's not funny!

DORIS
Aren't you pleased?

GEORGE
Pleased? It reminds me of my seventh birthday!

DORIS
What?

GEORGE
My uncle gave me fifty cents. I ran two miles and when I got there the candy store was closed!

DORIS

(*Puzzled*)

But doesn't this solve your—problem?

GEORGE

(*Frustrated*)

The idea doesn't solve anything! It's the execution that counts!

DORIS

(*Pleased*)

I really got to you, huh?

GEORGE

(*Tightly*)

Excuse me.

(*Without another word, he marches to the piano, sits and aggressively launches into a Rachmaninoff concerto. Surprisingly, he plays extremely well. Not quite concert hall material but close enough to fool a lot of people.* DORIS *watches, absolutely astounded. She finally recovers enough to get out of her chair and move to the piano where she watches him with an incredulous expression*)

DORIS

(*Finally*)

That's incredible! Are you as good as I think you are?

(*He continues to play until indicated*)

GEORGE
How good do you think I am?

DORIS
Sensational.

GEORGE
I'm not as good as you think I am.

DORIS
You sound marvelous to me.

GEORGE

It's the story of my life, Doris. All the form and none of the
ability.

DORIS

(*Puzzled*)

But for ten years that piano has been sitting there and you
haven't touched it. Why tonight?

GEORGE

It beats a cold shower.

DORIS

You play to release sexual tension?

GEORGE

Any kind of tension. Any frustration in my life and I head
right for the piano.

(*A wry shrug*)

You don't even get this good without a lot of practice.

(DORIS *shakes her head in wonder*)

DORIS

George, you're full of surprises.

GEORGE

Yeah, I know—you live with a man for ten days but you
never really know him.

DORIS
Why didn't you tell me you played before?

GEORGE
I had other ways of entertaining you.

DORIS
Well, I always knew you had wonderful hands.

(*He stops playing, looks at her*)

GEORGE
Look, lady, I only work here. I'm not allowed to date the customers.

(*She smiles, moves away. He starts playing again*)

DORIS
George? You still feel—frustrated?

GEORGE
I have the feeling it's going to take all six Brandenburg concertos.

DORIS
You'll be exhausted.

GEORGE
That's the idea.

DORIS
But—

GEORGE

(*Irritably*)

Doris, I've been waiting three months for—for the balloon
to go up! Well, it's up and it's not going to come down
until something—

DORIS
Honey, come here.

(*He stops playing, looks at her*)

Come on.

(*He gets up from the piano and moves to her. She starts
to untie his robe*)

GEORGE
Doris—

DORIS
It's okay. It'll be okay.

GEORGE
But you can't—

DORIS
I know that.

GEORGE
Then how—

DORIS
Don't worry, darling. We'll work something out.

(She kisses him very tenderly. Gradually he becomes more involved in the kiss until they are in a passionate embrace. Suddenly she backs away, clutching her stomach, her face a mixture of surprise and alarm. Then she grimaces with pain)

GEORGE

(Alarmed)

What is it?

(She is too busy fighting off the pain to answer)

Doris?

(The pain has knocked the breath out of her and she gasps to catch her breath)

Doris, for God's sake, what is it?

(She looks at him unbelievingly, not saying anything)

Doris, what *the hell is the matter?*

DORIS

(Finally)

If—if memory serves me correctly—I just had a labor pain.

(He stands stock still, trying to absorb this)

GEORGE
You—you can't have!

(*Clutching at straws*)

Maybe it's indigestion.

DORIS
No, there's a difference.

GEORGE
How can you be *sure?*

DORIS
I've had both.

GEORGE
But you can't be in labor! When is the baby due?

DORIS
Not for another month.

(*He stares at her for a moment and then puts his hands to his head*)

GEORGE
My God, what have I *done?!*

DORIS
What have *you* done?

GEORGE
I brought it on. My—my selfishness.

DORIS
George, don't be ridiculous. You had nothing to do with it.

GEORGE
Don't treat me like a child, Doris!

DORIS
Will you stop getting so excited?

GEORGE
Excited? I thought I had troubles before. Can you imagine what *this* is going to do to my sex life?

DORIS
George, will you—

(*She stops*)

I think I'd better—sit down.

(*He quickly moves to her, leads her to a chair*)

GEORGE

(*Anguished*)

Jesus, what kind of a man am I? What kind of man would do a thing like that?

DORIS
George, may I say something?

GEORGE

(*Very agitated—moving around*)

Look, I appreciate what you're trying to do, honey, but nothing you can say will make me feel any better.

DORIS
I'm not trying to make you feel any better.

(*This stops him in his tracks*)

GEORGE
What are you trying to say?

DORIS
We're in a lot of trouble. I'm going to have a baby.

GEORGE
I know that.

DORIS
I mean now. I have a history of short labor and—

(*She stops as another labor pain starts*)

GEORGE
Oh, Jesus!

(*He quickly moves to her, kneels in front of her and she grabs his hand in a viselike grip as she fights off the pain*)

Oh, Jesus!

(*The pain starts to subside*)

How—how do you feel?

DORIS
Like—like I'm going to have a baby.

GEORGE
Maybe it's a false alarm. It has to be a false alarm!

DORIS
Honey, try and get a hold of yourself. Get on the phone
and find out where the nearest hospital is.

GEORGE
Hospital? You want to go to a hospital?

DORIS
George, like it or not, I'm going to have a baby.

GEORGE
But we're not married!

(*She stares at him*)

I mean it's going to look—odd!

(*She gets up*)

DORIS
Get on the phone, George.

(*Moving towards the bathroom*)

And make sure you get the directions.

GEORGE
Where are you going?

DORIS
The bathroom.

GEORGE
Why?

DORIS
I don't have time to answer questions!

(*She exits to bathroom.*
He quickly moves to telephone, frantically jiggles
receiver bar)

GEORGE

(*Into phone*)

Hello, Mr. Chalmers? George. Can you tell me where the nearest hospital is?—Well, it's my—my wife. Something—unexpected came up. She got pregnant and now she's going to have the baby—How far is that?

(*With alarm*)

Oh, my God!—Get—get them on the phone for me, will you?

(*He covers receiver with hand, calls out*)

Are you okay, Doris?

(*There is no answer. Panicking*)

Doris! Doris, answer me!

DORIS

(*Offstage from bathroom—obviously in pain*)

In—a minute. I'm—busy.

GEORGE
Oh, Jesus.

(*Into phone*)

Hello—Hello, I'm staying at the Sea Shadows Inn just
outside Mendocino and—I—I heard this—this groaning
from—the next room. Well, I knocked on the door and
found this—this lady—who I'd never met before, in labor
and—Do *you* have to know that?—I still don't see
why—Okay, George Peterson!—Well, I didn't time it
exactly but—About three or four minutes I think—Hold
on.

(*Calling out*)

Doris, who's your doctor?

DORIS

(*Offstage—with an effort*)

Doctor Joseph—Harrington. Oakland. 555-78-78.

GEORGE

(*Into phone*)

Doctor Joseph Harrington in Oakland. His number is
555-7878—Yes, I have a car and I'm certainly willing to
help out if—I'll get her there—Right, right—Uh, could
you answer one question?—Would—uh—erotic contact
during pregnancy be the cause of premature—No reason, I
just wondered and—Right, I'll do that!

(*He hangs up, calls out*)

They're phoning your doctor. He'll meet us there at the
hospital.

(DORIS *appears in the doorway of the bathroom, a
strange look on her face. She doesn't say anything*)

Doris, did you hear me?

DORIS
I don't think we're going to make it to the hospital.

(*The blood drains from his face*)

GEORGE
What?

DORIS
My water just burst.

GEORGE
Oh, dear God.

DORIS
We're going to have to find a doctor in the area.

GEORGE
But supposing we *can't!*

DORIS
You look terrible. You're not going to faint, are you?

GEORGE

  (*In total shock*)

Doris, I'm not a cab driver! I don't know how to deliver babies!

DORIS
George, this is no time to start acting like Butterfly McQueen.

  (*She heads toward the bed*)

Get the nearest doctor on the phone.

  (*He races back to phone as she half sits and half lies on the bed*)

GEORGE

  (*Into phone*)

Who's the nearest doctor?—Get him on the phone! Fast! This is an emergency!

  (DORIS *has gone into another labor spasm.*
    GEORGE, *phone in hand, moves to her, puts his arm around her, grabs her hand*)

It's okay—hold on. Hold on. Doris. Hold on. There—
there—hold on. You okay?

DORIS

(*Weakly*)

This'll—teach you to fool around—with a married
woman.

(*Blurting*)

George, I'm scared!

GEORGE
You're going to be okay. Everything—

(*Into phone*)

Yes?

(*Standing up—yelling*)

His answering service! You don't understand. She's in
the last stages of labor!—Well, get in your car and drive
down to the goddam course! Just *get* him!

(*He hangs up*)

It's okay—he's on the golf course but it's just down the
road. Chalmers is getting him.

(DORIS *is staring at him with a look of total panic*)

Doris, what is it?

DORIS
I—I—can feel the baby!!

(*He stares at her, absorbs the situation, and we see a definite transformation take place. He rolls up the sleeves of his robe*)

GEORGE

(*Calmly*)

All right, lean back and try to relax. I'll be right back.

(*He exists quickly to the bathroom*)

DORIS

(*Screaming*)

George, don't leave me!

GEORGE

(*Offstage*)

Hold on, baby.

DORIS
George!

(*He reappears with a pile of towels*)

GEORGE
It's okay, I'm here. It'll be all right.

DORIS
What—are those—for?

GEORGE
Honey, we're going to have a baby.

DORIS
We?

GEORGE
Right. But I'm going to need your help.

(*She goes into a spasm of labor and he sits on the bed beside her*)

Okay—bear down—bear down. Come on, baby.

(*The lights start to fade*)

You're going to be fine. Just fine. You think I play the piano well? Wait until you get a load of how I deliver babies.

(*The lights have faded and the stage is dark*)

END OF ACT I, SCENE 3

ACT II

SCENE 1

THE TIME:
A day in February, 1965.

THE PLACE:
The same.

AT RISE:
GEORGE is unpacking his suitcase. Thinner than the last
time we saw him, he is wearing an expensive conservative
suit, his hair is gray and is worn unfashionably short. His
manner is more subdued than before and he looks and acts
older than his years. The door opens and DORIS bursts into
the room. She is wearing a brightly colored granny gown,
beads, sandals, and her hair is long and flowing. She is
carrying a decal decorated duffel bag.

DORIS
Hey, baby! What do ya say?

> (*She throws her duffel bag into a chair and herself into
> the arms of a very surprised* GEORGE. *She kisses him
> passionately, backs off and looks at him*)

So—you wanta fuck?

> (*He takes an astonished moment to absorb this*)

GEORGE

(*Finally*)

What?

DORIS

(*Grins*)

You didn't understand the question?

GEORGE
Of course I did. I just think it's a damned odd way to start a conversation.

DORIS
Yeah? I've always found it to be a great little icebreaker. Besides, I thought you might be feeling horny after your flight.

(GEORGE *continues to eye* DORIS *with a mild consternation*)

GEORGE
I didn't fly, I drove.

DORIS
From Connecticut?

GEORGE
From Los Angeles. We moved to Beverly Hills about ten months ago.

(He manages to yank his eyes away from (to him) DORIS'
bizarre appearance and resumes hanging up his clothes)

DORIS
How come?

GEORGE
Oh, a number of reasons.

(Shrugs)

I got fed up standing knee-deep in snow trying to scrape
the ice off my windshield with a credit card. Besides, there
are a lot of people out here with a lot of money who don't
know what to do with it.

DORIS
And you tell them?

GEORGE
I'm what they call a Business Manager.

DORIS
Things going okay?

GEORGE
I can't complain. Why?

DORIS
Because you look shitty.

(He turns to look at her)

Are you all right, honey?

GEORGE
I'm fine.

DORIS
You sure there's not something bothering you?

GEORGE
Yes—you. Do you always go around dressed like a bad finger painting?

DORIS

(*Grinning*)

No. I have to admit that today I am a little—well— visually overstated.

GEORGE
Why?

DORIS
I guess I wanted to make sure you knew you were dealing with the "new me." Sort of "show and tell."

GEORGE
You look like a refugee from Sunset Strip.

DORIS
Berkeley. I went back to school.

GEORGE

(*Bewildered*)

What for?

DORIS

(*Grins*)

You mean what do I want to be when I grow up?

GEORGE
Well, you have to admit it's a bit strange becoming a schoolgirl at your age.

DORIS
Are you kidding? Listen, it's not easy being the only one in the class with clear skin.

(*She moves to get her duffel bag, unpacks it through the following*)

GEORGE

(*Sitting*)

What made you do it?

DORIS
It was a dinner party that finally pushed me into it. Harry's boss invited us for dinner and I panicked.

GEORGE
Why?

DORIS
I'd spent so much time with kids I didn't know if I was capable of carrying on an intelligent conversation with anyone over five who wasn't a supermarket check-out clerk. Anyway, I went and was seated next to *the* boss. Well, I

surprised myself. He talked—then I talked—you know, just like a real conversation. I was feeling real cool until I noticed him looking at me in a weird way. I looked down and realized that all the time we'd been talking I'd been cutting up the meat on his plate. At that moment I *knew* I had to get out of the house.

GEORGE
But why school?

   (*She stretches out on the bed*)

DORIS
It's hard to explain. I felt restless and—undirected and I thought an education might give me some answers.

GEORGE
What sort of answers?

DORIS

   (*Shrugs*)

To find out where it's really at.

GEORGE

   (*Gets up*)

Jesus.

DORIS
What's the matter?

GEORGE
That expression.

DORIS
Okay. To find out who the hell I was.

GEORGE
You don't get those sort of answers from a classroom.

DORIS
I'm not in the classroom all the time. The demonstrations are a learning experience in themselves.

GEORGE
Demonstrations against what?

DORIS
The war of course. Didn't you hear about it? It was in all the papers.

GEORGE

(*Curtly*)

Demonstrations aren't going to stop the war.

DORIS
You have a better idea?

GEORGE
Look, I didn't come up here to discuss politics.

DORIS
Well, so far you've turned down sex and politics. You want to try religion?

GEORGE
I think I'll try a librium.

(*She watches him as he takes pill out and moves to take it with a glass of water from the drink tray*)

DORIS
George, why are you so uptight?

GEORGE
That's another expression I hate.

DORIS
Uptight?

GEORGE
There's no such word.

DORIS
You remind me of when I was nine years old and I asked my mother what "fuck" meant. Know what she said? "There's no such word."

GEORGE
And now you've found out there is you feel you have to use it in every other sentence?

DORIS
George, what's bugging you?

GEORGE
Bugging me? I'll tell you what's "bugging" me. The blacks

are burning down the cities, there's a Harvard professor telling my children the only way to happiness is to become a doped up zombie, and I have a teen-age son with hair so long that from the back he looks exactly like Yvonne de Carlo.

DORIS

(*Grins*)

That's right, baby—let it all hang out.

GEORGE

I wish people would *stop* letting it "all hang out." Especially my daughter. It's a wonder she hasn't been arrested for indecent exposure.

DORIS

That's a sign of age, honey.

GEORGE

What is?

DORIS

Being worried about the declining morality of the young. Besides, there's nothing you can do about it.

GEORGE

We could start by setting some examples.

DORIS

What are you going to do, George? Bring back public flogging?

GEORGE
It might not be a bad idea. We could start with the movie producers. My God, have you seen the films they're making today? Half the time the audience achieves a climax before the movies does!

DORIS
It's natural for people to be interested in sex. You can't kid the body, George.

GEORGE
Maybe not but you can damn well be *firm* with it.

   (*She giggles, gets off the bed, moves toward him*)

DORIS
When you were younger I don't remember you as being exactly a monk about that sort of thing.

GEORGE
That was different! Our relationship was not based upon a casual one night stand!

   (*She affectionately rumples his hair*)

DORIS
No, it's been *fifteen* one night stands.

GEORGE
It's not the same. We've *shared* things. My God, I helped deliver your child, remember?

DORIS
Remember? I think of it as our finest hour.

(She kisses him lightly, moves away to pour herself a drink)

GEORGE
How is she?

DORIS
Very healthy, very noisy and very spoiled.

GEORGE
You don't feel guilty about leaving her alone while you're at school?

DORIS
Harry's home a lot. The insurance business has been kind of slow lately.

GEORGE
How does he feel about all this?

DORIS
When I told him I wanted to go back to school because I want some identity he lost his temper and said, "You want identity? Go build a bridge! Invent penicillin but get off my back!"

GEORGE
I always said Harry had a good head on his shoulders.

DORIS
George, that was the *bad* story about him. How's Helen?

GEORGE
Helen's fine. Just fine.

DORIS
Tell me a story that shows how really lousy she can be.

GEORGE

(*Surprised*)

That's not like you.

DORIS
We seem to need something to bring us closer together.

GEORGE
I don't understand.

DORIS
I thought a really bad story about Helen might make you
appreciate me more.

(*This finally gets a small smile from* GEORGE)

GEORGE
Okay.

(*She sits with her drink and listens*)

As you know, she has this funny sense of humor.

DORIS
By funny I take it you mean peculiar?

GEORGE
Right. And it comes out at the most inappropriate times. I

had signed this client—very proper, very old money. Helen and I were invited out to his house for cocktails to get acquainted with him and his wife. Well, it was all pretty awkward but we managed to get through the drinks all right. Then as we went to leave, instead of walking out the front door I walked into the hall closet. Now that wasn't so bad—I mean anybody can do that. The mistake I made was that I *stayed* in there.

DORIS
You stayed in the closet?

GEORGE
Yes. I don't know—I guess I figured they hadn't noticed and I'd stay there until they'd gone away—okay, I admit I didn't think things through. I was in there for about a minute before I realized I'd—well—misjudged the situation. When I came out the three of them were just staring at me. All right, it was an embarrassing situation but I probably could have carried it off. Except for Helen. You know what she did?

DORIS
What?

GEORGE
She peed on the carpet.

DORIS

(*Incredulous*)

She did *what?*

GEORGE
Oh, not right away. First of all, she started to laugh. Her
face was all screwed up and the laughter was sort of—
squeaky. Then she held her stomach and tears started to
roll down her face. Then she peed on their Persian rug.

(DORIS *is having trouble keeping a straight face*)

DORIS
What did you say?

GEORGE
I said, "You'll have to excuse my wife. Ever since her last
pregnancy she's had a problem." Then I offered to have
the rug cleaned.

DORIS
Did that help?

GEORGE
They said it wasn't necessary. They had a maid.

(DORIS *finally explodes into peals of laughter*)

You think that's funny?

DORIS
I've been meaning to tell you this for years but I think I'd
like Helen.

GEORGE

(*Irritated*)

Would she come off any worse if I told you I lost the account?

DORIS
George, when did you get so *stuffy?*

GEORGE
Stuffy? Just because I don't like my wife urinating on my clients' carpets does not mean I'm stuffy!

DORIS
Okay, maybe not just that but—well—look at you.

(*She gets up, gestures at him*)

I mean—Jesus—you scream Establishment.

GEORGE
I am not a faddist!

DORIS
What's that mean?

GEORGE
I have no desire to be like those middle-aged idiots with bell bottom trousers and Prince Valiant haircuts who go around saying "Ciao."

DORIS
I wasn't talking about *fashion*. I was talking about your attitudes.

GEORGE
My attitudes are the same as they always were. I haven't changed at all.

DORIS
Yes, you have. You used to be crazy and—and insecure
and dumb and a terrible liar and—*human*. Now you seem
so *sure* of yourself.

GEORGE
That's the last thing I am.

(*She is surprised by his admission*)

DORIS
Oh?

(*He looks at her for a moment, frowns, moves to look
into the fire*)

GEORGE
I picked up one of Helen's magazines the other day and
there was this article telling women what quality of
orgasms they should have. It was called "The Big O."

(*He turns to face her*)

You know what really got to me? This was a magazine my
mother used to buy for its *fruit cake* recipes.

DORIS
The times they are a changing, darling.

GEORGE

(*Troubled*)

Too fast. I don't know, twenty, thirty years ago we were

brought up with standards—all right, they *were* blacks and
whites but they were standards. Today—it's so confusing.

DORIS
Well, that's at least a step in the right direction.

(*She moves to him and kisses him*)

GEORGE
When did I suddenly become so appealing?

DORIS
When you went from pompous to confused.

(*They kiss again*)

So what's your pleasure? A walk by the ocean, dinner, or
me?

GEORGE
You.

DORIS
Gee, I thought you'd never ask.

(*She steps back a pace and whips her dress off over her
head revealing that she is just wearing a pair of bikini
panties*)

GEORGE
My God.

DORIS
What is it?

GEORGE
Doris—you're not wearing a *bra!*

(*She giggles, embraces him*)

DORIS
Oh, George, you're so *forties.*

(*She starts to nibble on his ear*)

GEORGE

(*Becoming passionate*)

I happen to be an old-fashioned—man.

DORIS
The next thing you'll be telling me you voted for
Goldwater.

GEORGE
I did.

(*She takes a step back from him*)

DORIS
Are you putting me on?

GEORGE
Of course not.

(*Without another word, she picks up her dress and puts
it on*)

What—what are you doing?

DORIS

(*Furious*)

If you think I'm going to bed with any son of a bitch who voted for Goldwater you've got another think coming!

GEORGE
Doris, you can't do this to me! Not *now!*

DORIS
Oh, can't I? I'll tell you something—not only will I not go to bed with you—I want fifteen years of fucks back!

GEORGE
Doris, this is a very *delicate mechanism!!*

(*She stares at him unbelievingly*)

DORIS
My God, how could you vote for a man like that?

GEORGE

(*Moving toward her*)

Could we talk about this later?

DORIS

(*Pushing him away*)

No, we'll talk about it *now!* Why?

GEORGE

   (*Frustrated—yelling*)

Because I have a son who wants to be a rock musician!!

DORIS
What kind of reason is *that?*

GEORGE

   (*Sitting*)

The best reason I can come up with right now in my
condition!

DORIS
Well, you're going to have to do a lot better!

GEORGE
Okay, he was going to end the war!

DORIS
By bombing the hell out of innocent people!

GEORGE
What innocent people? They're *Reds!*

DORIS
They just wanted their country back!

GEORGE
Oh, I'm sick of hearing all that liberal crap! We've got the H bomb. Why don't we use it!

DORIS
Are you serious?

GEORGE
Yes, I'm serious. Wipe the sons of bitches off the face of the earth!

(*She stares at him for a moment*)

DORIS

(*Quietly, incredulous*)

My God, I don't know anything about you. What sort of a man are you?

GEORGE
Right now—very frustrated.

DORIS
All this time I thought you were a liberal Democrat. You told me you worked for Stevenson.

GEORGE

(*In a tired voice*)

That was years ago.

DORIS
What changed you? What happened to you?

GEORGE

(*Bitterly*)

I grew up.

DORIS
Yeah, well in my opinion you didn't turn out too well.

GEORGE
Let's forget it, huh?

DORIS
Forget it? How can I forget it? I mean being stuffy and—and old-fashioned is one thing but being a Fascist is another!

GEORGE

(*Flaring*)

I am not a Fascist!

DORIS
You're advocating mass murder!

GEORGE
Doris—drop it, okay! Just—drop it!

DORIS
How could you *do* this to me? Why, you stand for everything I'm against!

GEORGE
Then maybe you're against the wrong things!

DORIS
You used to think the same way I did.

GEORGE
I changed!

DORIS
Why?

GEORGE
Because Michael was killed! How the hell else did you expect me to feel!!

(*There is a long pause as she stands transfixed, trying to absorb this*)

DORIS

(*Finally*)

Oh—dear—God. How?

GEORGE
He was trying to get a wounded man onto a Red Cross helicopter and a sniper killed him.

(*Without a word, she moves to him, starts to put her arms around him.*
He brushes her away, rises and moves to window and stares out)

DORIS

(*Finally—almost in a whisper*)

When?

(*There is a pause*)

GEORGE

(*Dispassionately*)

We heard in the middle of a big July 4th party. Helen went completely to pieces—I'll never forget it. I didn't feel a thing. I thought I was in shock and it would hit me later.

(*He turns to face her*)

But you know something? It never did. The only emotion I can feel is blind anger. I didn't shed a tear.

(*She doesn't say anything*)

Isn't that the darnedest thing? I can't cry over my own son's death. I loved him but—for the life of me—I can't seem to cry over him.

(*She doesn't move as he crosses to shakily pour himself a drink*)

Doris, I'm sorry about—everything. Lately I've been a bit on edge and—

(The glass slips out of his hand, he tries to save it but it hits the dresser and smashes)

Oh, great! Will you look at that—I've gone and cut myself. If it isn't—one—damn thing—after—

(He starts to sob. DORIS *moves to him and puts her arms around him. He sinks into a chair, and buries his head into her chest as the curtain falls)*

END OF ACT II, SCENE 1

SCENE 2

THE TIME:
A day in February, 1970.

THE PLACE:
The same.

AT RISE:
DORIS AND GEORGE are lying on top of the rumpled bed
lazily enjoying the afterglow of lovemaking. GEORGE is
wearing jeans with a butterfly on the seat and longish hair.
His manner reflects a slightly self-conscious inner serenity.
DORIS is wearing an attractive kimono but during the scene
will don clothes and makeup that will project an image of
chic, expensive, good taste.

DORIS
It's amazing how good it can be after all these years, isn't
it?

GEORGE
All these years? Honey, if you add up all the times we've
actually made it together we're still on our honeymoon.

   (*A slight pause*)

DORIS
George, did you know I'm a grandmother?

GEORGE
No, but I think you picked a weird time to announce it.

DORIS
You think it's decadent having sex with a grandmother?

GEORGE
Only if it's done well.

(*He pats her hand*)

Anyway, you're the youngest looking grandmother I've ever had a peak experience with.

DORIS

(*Getting off bed*)

My mother thanks you, my father thanks you, my hairdresser thanks you and my plastic surgeon thanks you.

(*He watches her as she lights a cigarette, sits at dresser, peers into mirror, starts to brush hair and apply makeup*)

When Harry says, "You're not the girl I married," he doesn't know how right he is.

GEORGE
Didn't Harry like your old nose?

DORIS
He thinks this *is* my old nose.

GEORGE
He never noticed?

DORIS

(*Flippantly*)

Pathetic, isn't it? A new dress I could understand—but a whole nose?

GEORGE
Well, to be totally honest I really can't see much of a difference either.

DORIS
Who cares? It looks different from *my* side. Makes me *act* more attractive.

GEORGE
Why do you feel you need a validation of your attractiveness?

DORIS

(*A slight shrug*)

A woman starts feeling a little insecure when she gets to be forty-four.

GEORGE
Forty-five.

DORIS
See what I mean? Anyway, that's this year's rotten story about Harry. Got one about Helen?

(He grins, gets off bed, dons shirt, denim jacket and sandals during the following)

GEORGE

There was a loud party next door. Helen couldn't sleep and she didn't want to take a sleeping pill because she had to get up at six the next morning. So she stuffed two pills in her ears. During the night they melted. The next morning as the doctor was digging the stuff out of her ears he said, "You know these *can* be taken orally." Helen just laughed.

DORIS

If that's the worst story you can tell about her you must be a very happy man.

(He sits on the piano bench)

GEORGE

Well, let's say I've discovered I have the *potential* for happiness.

(The phone rings. DORIS immediately moves to answer it)

DORIS

(Into phone)

Hello.

(Just a hint of disappointment)

Oh, hi, Liz. No, it's sixty—not sixteen guests—That's right—a brunch— We've catered a couple of parties for her

before—No problem. She sets up tables around the pool
and there's room for the buffet on the patio—Right.
Anyone else call?—Okay, I'll be at this number.

(*She hangs up, turns to* GEORGE, *who has been watching
her*)

Sorry, busy weekend. I had to leave the number.

GEORGE
Does Harry know you're here?

DORIS
No, he still thinks I go on the retreat. Don't worry.

(*She moves and proceeds to get dressed during the
following*)

GEORGE
I'm not worried.

DORIS
Then why are you frowning?

GEORGE
I'm getting some bad vibes again.

DORIS
Again?

GEORGE
When you first walked into the room I picked up on your
high tension level. Then after we made love I sensed a
certain anxiety reduction but now I'm getting a definite
negative feedback.

DORIS
How long you been in analysis?

GEORGE
How did you know I was in analysis?

DORIS

(*Drily*)

Just a wild guess. What made you go into therapy?

GEORGE

(*With a shrug*)

My value system changed.

(*He casually plays some soft, pleasant chords at the piano as he talks*)

One day I took a look at my $150,000 house, the three cars in the garage, the swimming pool, and the gardeners and I thought—"*Why?*" I mean did I really want the whole status trip? So—I decided to try and find out what I did want and who I was.

DORIS
And you went from analysis to Esalen to Gestalt to Transactional to encounter groups to Nirvana.

(*He stops playing, swivels to face her, speaks in a calm, reasonable voice*)

GEORGE
Doris, just because many people are trying to expand their emotional horizons doesn't make the experience any less valid. I've learned a lot.

DORIS
I've noticed. For one thing you learned to talk as if you're reasoning with someone about to jump off a skyscraper ledge.

GEORGE

(*Grins*)

Okay—okay. I know I tend to overcompensate for my emotionalism and sometimes there's a certain loss of spontaneity. I'm working on that.

DORIS
I'm glad to hear it. What else did you find out?

GEORGE

(*Simply*)

That behind the walls I've built around myself I'm a warm, caring, loving human being.

(*She looks at him for a moment*)

DORIS
I could have told you that twenty years ago. How does Helen feel about this "voyage of self discovery"?

GEORGE
At first she tended to overact.

DORIS
In what way?

GEORGE
She threw a grapefruit at me in the Thriftimart. It was
natural that we'd have some interpersonal conflicts to work
through but now it's cool. She's into pottery.

DORIS
But how do you make a living?

GEORGE
We live very simply, Doris—we don't need much. What
bread we do need I can provide by simple, honest labor.

DORIS
Like what?

GEORGE
I play cocktail piano in a singles bar in the Valley.

(*The phone rings again.* DORIS *quickly moves to answer
it*)

DORIS

(*Into phone*)

Hello—Oh, hi, Liz—No way. Tell him that's our final
offer—I don't care how good a location it is—That's bull,
Liz, he needs us more than we need him. If he doesn't like

it he can shove it but don't worry—he won't. Anything
else?—Okay, you know the number.

(*She hangs up*)

I'm buying another store.

GEORGE
Why?

DORIS
Money.

(*She continues to dress*)

GEORGE
Is that why you went into business? Just to make money?

DORIS
Of course not. I wanted money *and* power. And it finally
penetrated my thick little head that attending C.R. groups
with ten other frustrated housewives wasn't going to change
anything.

GEORGE
C.R. groups?

DORIS
Consciousness raising.

(*He nods*)

I take it you *are* for Women's Liberation?

GEORGE

Listen, I'm for any kind of liberation.

DORIS

That's a cop out. Women have always been exploited by men and you know it.

GEORGE

We've *all* been shafted, Doris, and by the same things.

(*He gets up*)

Look, let me lay this on you. I go to a woman doctor. The first time she gave me a rectal examination she said, "Am I hurting you or are you tense?" I said, "I'm tense." Then she said, "Are you tense because I'm a woman?" and I said, "No, I get tense when *anybody* does that to me."

(*A beat*)

You see what I mean?

DORIS

I don't know but I *do* know that the only time a woman is taken seriously in this country is when she has the money to back up her mouth. The business has given me that.

GEORGE

(*Mildly*)

Well, I guess it's nice to have a hobby.

DORIS
Hobby? We grossed over half a million dollars the first year.

GEORGE
Honey, if that's what you want I'm very happy for you.

(*A slight shrug*)

It's just that I'm not into the money thing anymore.

(*She looks at him for a moment*)

DORIS

(*Lightly*)

George, you ever get the feeling we're drifting apart?

GEORGE
No. In many ways I've never felt closer to you.

DORIS
Really? I don't know, sometimes I think our lives are always—out of sync.

GEORGE
We all realize our potential in different ways at different times. All I ask is that you don't lay *your* trip on me, that's all.

(*She moves to purse, extracts check*)

DORIS
Then let me lay this on you.

(*She hands him check*)

Here—it's the money you loaned me to start the store.

GEORGE

(*Looking at check*)

It's three times the amount I gave you.

DORIS
Return on your investment.

GEORGE
I can't accept this, Doris.

DORIS

(*Firmly*)

You can and you will. I'm not going to have any lover of mine playing piano in a singles bar. Sounds tacky.

(*They smile at one another*)

GEORGE
You never used to order me around.

DORIS
I've come a long way, baby.

GEORGE
The important thing is does it give you a sense of
fulfillment?

DORIS
Fulfillment? Let me tell you about fulfillment.

(*She moves to finish dressing*)

I went into Gucci's the other day and I noticed a suede suit
I liked and asked one of their snotty salesgirls the price. She
said, "Seven hundred dollars," and started to walk away. I
said, "I'll take five." She turned and said, "Five? Why on
earth would you want five?" and I said, "I want them for
my bowling team." *That's* fulfillment.

GEORGE
So you have everything you want?

DORIS

(*Lighting cigarette—flippantly*)

With one minor exception. Somewhere along the way I
seem to have lost my husband.

GEORGE
Lost him?

DORIS
Well, I don't know if I've lost him or simply misplaced
him. He walked out of the house four days ago and I
haven't heard from him since.

GEORGE
How do you feel about that?

DORIS
George, do me a favor—stop acting as if you're leading a human potential group. It really pisses me off.

GEORGE
That's cool.

DORIS
What's cool?

GEORGE
For you to transfer your hostility and feelings of aggression from Harry to me. As long as you *know* that's what you're doing.

DORIS
You mind if I tell you something, George? You're beginning to get on my nerves.

GEORGE
That's cool too.

DORIS
Jesus.

GEORGE
I mean it. At least it's *honest*. That's the key to everything —total honesty.

DORIS
Oh really? And are you totally honest with Helen?

GEORGE
I'm trying.

DORIS
Have you told her about us?

GEORGE
No—but I could.

(*She grimaces*)

Really, I think that today she's matured enough to handle it.

DORIS
George, you're full of shit.

GEORGE
I can buy that—if you're really being *honest.*

DORIS
Believe me, I'm being honest!

GEORGE
Well, at least it's a start. But what about that other garbage?

(*She starts to speak*)

Oh come on, Doris!

(*Imitating her*)

"I don't know if I lost him or simply misplaced him." I mean what sort of crap is that?

(She looks at him for a moment)

DORIS
Okay, you have a point.

GEORGE
Is there someone else?

DORIS
I don't think so. I *know* there isn't with me.

(Getting agitated)

That's what really gets to me. Did you know I've been married for over twenty-five years and I've never cheated on him *once!*

(He doesn't say anything)

Well, you know what I mean.

GEORGE
What is it then? Boredom?

DORIS
No. Oh, Harry's not exactly Cary Grant anymore but then neither is Cary Grant.

GEORGE
So how do you feel about all this?

DORIS
You're doing it again, George.

(*He doesn't say anything*)

Okay, I think—

GEORGE
No, don't tell me what you think. Tell me what you *feel*.

DORIS
Like I've been kicked in the stomach.

GEORGE
That's good.

(*She looks at him*)

What else?

DORIS
Angry, hurt, betrayed and—okay, a little guilty. But you know something? I *resent* the fact that he's made me feel guilty.

GEORGE
Why do you feel resentment?

DORIS

(*Angrily*)

Look, I didn't marry Harry because he had a head for business! Okay, it so happens that I discovered *I* did. Or maybe I was just lucky—I don't know. The point is, I don't love Harry any less because he's a failure as a provider. Why should he love me any less because I'm a success?

(He doesn't say anything, she sighs)

I don't know—one of these days I'm going to know exactly how I *do* feel.

GEORGE
You don't know?

DORIS
It varies between Joan of Arc, Rosalind Russell and Betty Crocker.

GEORGE
Well, I suppose most women are going through a transitional period.

DORIS

(With a wry grimace)

Yeah, but what am I going to do tonight?

GEORGE
Have you told him you still love him?

DORIS
Love him? Why does he think I've been hanging around with him for twenty-seven years?

GEORGE

(In his calm, reasonable voice)

I just mean that right now his masculinity is being

threatened and he probably needs some validation of his
worth as a man.

DORIS
And how the hell do I do all that? I mean that's *some* trick.

GEORGE
Total honesty, Doris. Is it so hard for you to tell him that
you understand how he feels?

DORIS
Right now—it is, yes.

GEORGE
Oh?

DORIS
I mean why the hell should I apologize for doing something
well? It's *his* ego that's screwed us up. I mean I really
resent that!

GEORGE
You want him back?

DORIS
Right at this moment I'm not sure I do. Ask me tomorrow
and I'll probably give you a different answer.

GEORGE
Why?

DORIS

(*Simply*)

Tomorrow I won't have you.

GEORGE
I'm always with you in spirit.

DORIS
It's not easy to spiritually put your cold feet on someone's back.

GEORGE
Is that a proposal, Doris?

DORIS
You interested?

GEORGE
Are you?

DORIS
For two cents.

GEORGE
Leave Helen and Harry?

DORIS
Sure. Present a united back.

(*He is looking at her, trying to determine whether she's serious*)

Don't look so panicky, George. I'm only three quarters serious.

(*There is a pause*)

GEORGE
Well, when you have your head together and are
completely serious why don't you ask me again.

DORIS
I bet you say that to all the girls.

GEORGE
No.

(*She cups his face in her hands and kisses him*)

DORIS
Thanks.

GEORGE
And stop feeling so insecure.

DORIS
About what?

GEORGE
You're as feminine as you always were.

[(*She looks at him for a moment*)

DORIS
I know Gloria Steinem would hate me but I'm glad you
said that.

(*She gives a little shrug*)

I guess I'm not as emancipated as I thought I was.

GEORGE
None of us are.

(*She grins at him*)

DORIS
You hungry?

GEORGE
Yes.

DORIS
Well, you're a lucky man because tonight our dinner is being catered by the chicest, most expensive French delicatessen in San Francisco.

GEORGE
How'd we swing that?

DORIS
The owner has a thing about you.

(*As she moves toward the door*)

It's all in the trunk of my car.

GEORGE
You need any help?

DORIS
Yes. Set the table, light the candles, and when I come back make me laugh.

GEORGE
I'll try.

DORIS
That's okay. If you can't make me laugh just hold my hand.

(*She exits.*
He moves to prepare the table for the food. The phone rings. He hesitates for a moment before picking up the receiver)

GEORGE

(*Into the phone*)

Hello—No, she's not here right now. Who is this?

(*His face freezes*)

Harry!—Uh, hold—hold on a moment.

(*He places the phone on the floor, stares at it for a moment. Then he paces in a circle around it, his mind wrestling with the alternatives. He stops, stares at it, takes a deep breath, picks up the receiver*)

Hello—Harry, we're two adult, mature human beings and I've decided to be totally honest with you—No, Doris is not here right now but *I'd* like to talk to you—Because I know you and Doris have been having a rough time lately and —We're very close friends. I've known Doris for twenty years and through her I feel as if I know you—Well, we've been meeting this same weekend for twenty years—The

Retreat? Well, we can get into that later but first I want
you to know something. She loves you, Harry—she really
loves you—I just know, Harry—Look, maybe if I told you
a story she just told me this morning it would help you
understand. A few months ago Doris was supposed to act as
a den mother for your ten-year-old daughter Georgina and
her Indian guide group. Well, she got hung up at the store
and was two hours late getting home. When she walked
into the house she looked into the living room and do you
know what she saw? A rather overweight, balding,
middle-aged man with a feather on his head sitting
cross-legged on the floor very gravely and gently telling a
circle of totally absorbed little girls what it was like to be in
a World War II Japanese prison camp. She turned around,
walked out of the house, sat in her car and thanked God
for being married to a man like you—Are you still there,
Harry?—Well, sometimes married people get into an
emotional straitjacket and find it difficult to communicate
how they truly feel about each other. Honesty is the key to
everything—Yes, we've had a very close, very intimate
relationship for twenty years and I'm not ashamed to admit
that it's been one of the most satisfying experiences of my
life—My name? My name is Father Michael O'Herlihy.

(*The lights start to dim as he keeps talking*)

No, she's out saying a novena right now—Yes, my son, I'll
tell her to call you.

(*The curtain has fallen*)

END OF ACT II, SCENE 2

SCENE 3

THE TIME:
A day in February, 1975.

THE PLACE:
The same.

AT RISE:
DORIS is alone on the stage silently mouthing "twenty-one, twenty-two, twenty-three" as she finishes transferring some red roses from a box into a silver vase. She is well dressed but her clothes are softer, more feminine and less fashionable than the last time we saw her. She turns as GEORGE enters. His hair has been trimmed to a "conservatively long" length and his raincoat covers his comfortably rumpled sports coat, pants, and turtle neck sweater. They drink one another in for a moment before they embrace affectionately.

GEORGE
You feel *good*.

DORIS
So do you.

(*She looks at him*)

But you *look* tired.

GEORGE

(*Grins*)

I've looked this way for years. You just haven't noticed.

(*She doesn't say anything but we see the concern in her eyes. He turns away, takes off his raincoat and throws it over a chair during the following*)

Anyway, I feel better now I'm here. This room's always had that effect on me.

DORIS
I know what you mean. I guess it proves that maybe you can't buy happiness but you can certainly *rent* it.

(*She gazes around the room affectionately*)

It never changes, does it?

GEORGE
About the only thing that doesn't.

DORIS
I find that comforting.

GEORGE
Even old Chalmers is the same. He must be seventy-five by now.

(*He smiles at her*)

Remember when we first met how even then we called him Old Chalmers?

(*She nods*)

He must have been about the same age we are now.

DORIS
That I don't find comforting.

GEORGE
We were very young.

(*They gaze at one another for a moment*)

DORIS
Have we changed, George?

GEORGE
Of course. I grew up with you. Remember the dumb lies I used to tell?

DORIS

(*Nods*)

I miss them.

GEORGE
I don't. It was no fun being that insecure.

DORIS
And what about me? Have I grown up too?

GEORGE
Oh, I have the feeling you were already grown up when I met you.

(They smile at one another)

Tell me something.

DORIS
Anything.

GEORGE
Why is it that every time I look at you I want to put my hands all over you?

(She moves to embrace him)

DORIS
That's another thing that hasn't changed. You always were a sex maniac.

GEORGE

(Nuzzling her)

Softest thing I've touched in months is Rusty, my cocker spaniel.

(She looks at him in surprise)

DORIS
Oh?

(He avoids the unspoken query by moving away to the fireplace)

GEORGE
Let's see if I can get this fire going.

(*She watches him as he throws another log on*)

You know I figured out with the cost of firewood today it's cheaper to buy Akron furniture, break it up, and burn *it*.

DORIS
Things that tight?

GEORGE
No, I'm okay. I've been doing some teaching at U.C.L.A.

DORIS
Music?

GEORGE
Accounting.

(*He shrugs, gestures at the window*)

It seems with everything that's happening out there figures are still the only things that don't lie.

(*She moves to pour two cups of coffee from a coffee pot that has been set up on a tray*)

Doris, why'd you sell your business?

DORIS

(*Surprised*)

How did you know that?

GEORGE
I'll tell you later. What made you do it?

DORIS
I was bought out by a chain.

(*A slight shrug*)

It was the right offer at the right time.

GEORGE
But I thought you loved working.

DORIS
Well, there was another factor. Harry had a heart
attack.

(*She hands him a cup of coffee*)

It turned out to be a mild one but he needed me to look
after him—so—

(*She shrugs*)

GEORGE
You don't miss the action?

DORIS
Not yet. I guess I'm still enjoying being one of the idle
rich.

(*He sits with his coffee as she moves to get a cup for
herself*)

GEORGE
But what do you do with yourself?

DORIS
Oh—read, watch TV, play a little golf, visit our grandchildren—you know, all the jet set stuff.

GEORGE
Harry's okay now?

(*She sits opposite him*)

DORIS
Runs four miles a day and has a body like Mark Spitz.

(*Grins*)

Unfortunately, his face is still like Ernest Borgnine's. You want to hear a nice story about him?

GEORGE

(*Unenthusiastically*)

Sure.

DORIS
Right after the heart attack when he came out of intensive care he looked up at the doctor and said, "Doc, give it to me straight. After I get out of the hospital will I be able to play the piano?" The doctor said, "Of course" and Harry said, "Funny, I couldn't play it *before*."

(GEORGE *gives a polite smile, gets up, moves to look out of the window*)

You don't understand—it wasn't that it was that funny. It's just that Harry *never* makes jokes but he saw how panicky I was and wanted to make me feel better.

GEORGE
Doris, how are you and Harry? You know—emotionally.

DORIS
Comfortable.

GEORGE
You're willing to settle for that?

(*She moves to pick up his raincoat*)

DORIS
Oh, it's not such a bad state. The word's been given a bad reputation by the young.

(*She looks around for his luggage*)

Where's your luggage? Still in the car?

GEORGE
I didn't bring any.

(*She looks at him*)

I—I can't stay, Doris.

DORIS

(*Puzzled*)

Why?

GEORGE
Look, I have a lot to say and a short time to say it so I'd
better start now.

(*She waits.
He takes a breath*)

First of all, Helen's known about us for over ten years.

DORIS

(*Finally*)

When did you find out?

GEORGE
Two months ago.

DORIS
She never confronted you with it before?

GEORGE
No.

(*She slowly sits*)

DORIS
I always wondered how we managed to pull it off. I guess
we didn't. What made her finally tell you?

GEORGE
She didn't. She has this—this old friend—Connie—maybe I've mentioned her before. She told me.

(*He shakes his head unbelievingly*)

All those years and Helen never even hinted that she knew.

(*A beat*)

I guess that's the nicest story I've ever told about her.

DORIS
Your wife's an amazing woman, George.

GEORGE
She's dead.

(*She just looks at him*)

She died six months ago. Cancer. It was all—very fast.

(*She slowly gets up, moves to look into the fire*)

I'm sorry to blurt it out like that. I just couldn't think of a—a graceful way to tell you.

(*She nods, her back still to him*)

You okay, honey?

DORIS
It's so strange. I never met Helen. But—but I feel as if I've just lost my best friend. It's—crazy.

(He doesn't say anything. She turns to face him)

It must have been awful for you.

GEORGE
You cope. You don't think you can but—you cope.

(She moves to him, touches his cheek with her hand)

DORIS
The kids okay?

GEORGE
They'll survive. I don't think I could have got through the whole thing without them.

(He moves away)

Then of course there was—Connie.

DORIS
Connie?

GEORGE
She'd lost her husband a few years ago so there was a certain—empathy.

DORIS
Oh?

GEORGE
She's a friend, Doris. A very good friend. We've always felt very—comfortable—together. I suppose it's because she's a lot like Helen.

(She reacts with a slight frown)

Is there something the matter?

DORIS
I just wish you'd tried to reach me.

GEORGE
I did. That's when I found out you'd sold the stores. I called and they gave me your home number. I let the phone ring four times, then I hung up. But it made me feel better knowing you were there if I needed you.

DORIS
I wish you'd spoken to me.

GEORGE
I didn't want to intrude. I didn't feel I had the right.

DORIS
My God, that's terrible. We should have been together.

GEORGE
I've been thinking about us a lot lately. Everything we've been through together. The things we shared. The times we've helped each other. Did you know we've made love a hundred and thirteen times? I figured it out on my Bomar calculator.

(He is fixing fresh cups of coffee)

It's a wonderful thing to know someone that well. You know, there is nothing about you I don't know. It's two sugars, right?

DORIS
No, one.

GEORGE
Cream?

(*She shakes her head*)

So, I don't know everything about you. I don't know who your favorite movie stars are and I couldn't remember the name of your favorite perfume. I racked my brain but I couldn't remember.

DORIS

(*Smiles*)

That's funny. It's My Sin.

GEORGE
But I do know that in twenty-four years I've never been out of love with you. I find that incredible. So what do you say, Doris, you want to get married?

DORIS

(*Lightly*)

Married? We shouldn't even be doing this.

GEORGE
I'm serious.

DORIS

(*Looking at him*)

You really are, aren't you?

GEORGE
What did you think I was—just another summer romance?
A simple "yes" will do.

DORIS
There's no such thing, George.

GEORGE
What is it?

DORIS
I was just thinking of how many times I've dreamed of you
asking me this. It's pulled me through a lot of bad times. I
want to thank you for that.

GEORGE
What did you say to me all those times?

DORIS
I always said "yes."

GEORGE
Then why are you hesitating now?

(*Pause*)

Do you realize I'm giving you the opportunity to marry **a** man who has known you for twenty-four years and every time you walk by still wants to grab your ass?

DORIS
You always were a sweet talker.

GEORGE
That's because if I told you how I really felt about you it would probably sound like a medley of clichés from popular songs. Will you marry me?

DORIS

(*Pause*)

I can't.

GEORGE
Why not?

DORIS
I'm already married.

GEORGE
You feel you have to stay because he needs you?

DORIS
No, it's more than that. George, try and understand.

(*She moves away and turns to him*)

When I look at Harry I don't only see the way he is now. I see all the other Harrys I've known. I'm sure he feels the same way about me. When we look at our children—our grandchildren—old movies on TV—anything—we share the same memories.

(*A beat*)

It's—comfortable. Maybe that's what marriage is all about in the end—I don't know.

(*A slight pause*)

Didn't you feel that way with Helen?

(*There is a short pause*)

GEORGE

(*Exploding*)

Goddamit!

(*He smashes his coffee cup into the fireplace*)

I was the one who got you back together three years ago! Why did I *do* a stupid thing like that! I mean why the hell was I so goddam generous!?

DORIS
Because you felt the same way about Helen then as I do about Harry now.

GEORGE
What's that got to do with anything?!

DORIS
If I hadn't gone back to Harry you might have been stuck
with me permanently and you were terrified.

(*He looks at her, manages a sheepish grin*)

GEORGE
You could always see through me, couldn't you?

DORIS
That's okay. I always liked what I saw.

GEORGE
Well, I want you now.

DORIS
I'm still available once a year.

(*He doesn't say anything*)

Same time, same place?

(*She catches a certain look in his eyes*)

What is it?

(*He looks at her for a moment, paces, turns to face her*)

GEORGE

(*Awkwardly*)

Doris—I—I need a wife. I'm just not the kind of man who
can live alone. I want you to marry me but when I came

here I—I knew there was an outside chance you'd say "no."
What I'm trying to say is—if you don't marry me I'll
probably end up marrying Connie. No—that's a lie—I will
marry her. She knows why I came here today. She
knows—all about you. The point is, she's not the sort of
woman who would go along with our—relationship.

(*A beat*)

You understand?

(DORIS *manages a nod*)

I suppose what I'm saying is that if you don't marry me we
won't ever see each other again.

(DORIS *is frozen, he moves to take her hand*)

You're trembling.

DORIS
The thought of never seeing you again terrifies me.

GEORGE
Doris, for God's sake—marry me!

DORIS

(*Finally—torn*)

I'm sorry—I can't.

(*He looks at her for a long moment*)

Don't hate me, George.

GEORGE
I could never hate you. I was just trying to think of something that would break your heart, make you burst into tears and come with me.

DORIS
You know us Italians. We never cry.

(*He makes a gesture of helplessness, stands*)

GEORGE
What time is it?

(*She holds out her wrist, he looks at her watch, reacts*)

Five-fifty-five.

DORIS
No, it's only two-thirty. I always keep my watch three hours and twenty-five minutes fast.

GEORGE

(*Puzzled*)

How long you been doing that?

DORIS
About twenty odd years.

GEORGE
Why would anyone want to do that?

DORIS
Personal idiosyncrasy.

(There is an awkward pause)

GEORGE
Well—I—I have a plane to catch.

(She nods, stands. They look at one another)

You know, I can't believe this is happening to us.

(She doesn't say anything)

Yeah. Well—

(They embrace and kiss, clumsily and awkwardly, almost like two strangers. They break, he picks up his raincoat, moves to door, turns to look at her)

GEORGE
Who were your favorite movie stars?

DORIS
Lon McAllister, Howard Keel, Cary Grant, Marlon Brando, and Laurence Olivier.

GEORGE
You've come a long way.

DORIS
We both have.

(He opens door, looks at her)

GEORGE
Always keep your watch three hours and twenty-five minutes fast, huh?

(*He exits quickly, shutting the door behind him.*
DORIS *stands for a moment trying to absorb the shock of his departure. Then, trancelike, she moves to the closet where she gets her suitcase, puts it on the sofa, and starts to pack but stops to look lovingly around the room, drinking in the memories before her eyes come to rest upon the vase of roses. She slowly moves to the roses, takes one out, closes her eyes and rests it gently against her cheek. She holds this pose for a long moment before her eyes jolt open as the door crashes open and* GEORGE, *perspiring and very agitated, bursts into the room, holding his suitcases. He drops his cases with a thump, fixes her with an angry, frustrated look*)

Okay, you win goddamit! You can't look a gift horse in the mouth!

DORIS

(*Astounded*)

But—but what about Connie?

GEORGE

(*Yelling*)

There is no Connie! I made her up!

(*She just stares at him, dumbfounded*)

No, that's a lie too. There is a Connie but she's sixty-nine years old!

(DORIS *is still speechless*)

Doris, I wanted you to *marry* me and I figured if you thought there was someone else you'd—okay, maybe I didn't think it through. I was desperate, okay?

(*Getting even more agitated*)

Look, for once in my life I wanted a happy ending, can't you understand that?! Listen, I don't want to talk about it anymore!

(*Still speechless she watches him march to the bed and start to furiously undress. He turns to look at her*)

Okay! You're right about that too! If you had married me we might have just ended up with a "comfortable" ending!

(*She opens her mouth to speak*)

Look, I'm in no mood to figure it out right now. All I know is I'm back and I'm going to keep coming back every year until our bones are too brittle to risk contact.

(*She starts to laugh, her laughter builds and then almost imperceptibly changes to something else and we realize that she is crying. She moves blindly into his arms, still sobbing. He gently tips her face up so that he can look at her and speaks very softly*)

After twenty-four years? Why now?

DORIS

(*Through her tears*)

Because I love—happy—endings!

(*He picks her up, places her on the bed and as he lies
beside her the lights slowly dim until there is just a pin
spot on the vase of roses. Finally, this too fades, the stage
is dark, and the play is over*)

THE END